THE NIGHTLIFE NEW YORK

TRAVIS LUEDKE

THE NIGHTLIFE: NEW YORK

Published by Travis Luedke

Copyright 2012 by Travis Luedke

Book Cover Art by Amygdala Design
http://amygdaladesign.net/

THIRD EDITION

ISBN-13: 978-1481948777
ISBN-10: 1481948776

Adult Reading Material (17+)
Contains scenes of graphic sex and violence
unsuitable for underage readers

This is a work of fiction. Names, characters, places, brands, media, and incidents are either the product of author's imagination or are used fictitiously. The author acknowledges the trademarked status and trademark owners of various products referenced in this work of fiction, which have been used without permission. The publication/use of these trademarks is not authorized, associated with, or sponsored by the trademark owners.

ACKNOWLEDGMENTS

This is the first novel I wrote. My virgin novel. The influences and help for this book came from so many sources, there's no way to begin to acknowledge all the people that had a hand. I had already written and rewritten Nightlife New York several times over when I found this wonderful place called 'ladieswhocritique.com.'

That's when I learned that I had only just begun to edit my novel. Three rewrites later, here it is, in its third edition.

I have to give heaping tons of praise and credit to my indispensable critique partners and editors, Patricia, Kayla, Marilyn, Michelle, and numerous other beta readers who gave me invaluable feedback. And there's this Canadian author, M. Joseph Murphy, who had the nerve to tell me my French was *off*. So I talked him into helping me fix it.

And, as always, I have to give credit to my mother, and my wife, who suffered through reading the first drafts of this novel, back when Michelle's accent was so bad even I couldn't understand what she was saying half the time. ☺

Regards,

Travis Luedke

CHAPTER 1

Dead on his feet and ready to clock out, Aaron Pilan didn't immediately react when Charlene groped a good handful of his ass. Burned out from a long, hard shift of waiting tables, Aaron's delayed reaction wasn't anything charming or witty as his boss Bemichi would have preferred. Refilling Charlene's merlot that he'd already refilled one too many times, he deadpanned, "Is there anything else I can do for you?" He realized too late, his question could easily have been misinterpreted as an encouragement to her advances.

He definitely didn't want to mislead or encourage Charlene. He found her attractive, with that "MILF" allure—*Mother I'd Like to Fuck*—of older more sophisticated women. But the problem with Charlene came two-fold. She was both a regular customer, and of sufficient age to actually be his mother. And she probably knew enough about sex to thoroughly corrupt his innocence, which, much to his chagrin, remained mostly intact.

The real reason he chose not to fraternize with customers was his ever-present fear of the wrath of Bemichi that could descend upon his shoulders like angels of judgment bearing fiery swords. His boss Antonio Bemichi, who owned the restaurant for two decades, wasn't one to allow such indiscretions to pass without consequence. Aaron had been warned his first day in training, "Hell hath no fury like an Italian restaurant proprietor scorned."

Bemichi, like many Italians in New York, took great pride in his fine dining establishment and customer service. After all, the place carried his namesake, *Bemichis Restaurant*. Like many Italians, Bemichi's fiery temper flared and screeched in a fountain fireworks display. Fortunately his tirades sputtered out just as quickly.

Aaron considered Bemichi a decent guy, and the job wasn't bad, the food even better. Aaron enjoyed his work … *most of the time*. The interior décor of Bemichis resembled a New York Italian version of the *Olive Garden* with comparable pricing. The kind of place to bring the whole family, slurp down all the fabulous Italian pastas, and then waddle home an hour later, wonderfully sated, without having emptied your wallet.

For Charlene, Bemichis held the added allure of hitting on waiters half her age, secure in the knowledge they would grin and bear it for propriety's sake. Aaron didn't complain, he'd gotten used to her hands on his ass. He suspected she patronized the restaurant for the express purpose of fondling him when her liquid courage was sufficiently wetted. She seemed to go after him at around the third refill of merlot. That should be her cutoff point, but then, he wasn't entirely averse to the occasional grope. Definitely not getting any at home. Besides, she always left a hefty tip—a consolation prize for putting his wares at her fingertips.

The game of grab-ass had grown old months ago. It was no longer surprising. At this late hour Aaron just wanted to finish his shift—*like now.* He watched the time tick by. The hands on the clock advanced in exaggerated slow motion, mocking him with their lazy movements. Twelve o'clock midnight arrived not a moment too soon. He moved so fast making his escape out the door, that he ignored the first call on his cell phone from his roommate Kyle. When Kyle called back seconds later, he figured he better answer, it must be important.

"Hey Kyle, what's up? I'm trying to get outta here."

"Hey guy, I gotta warn you." Kyle spoke over the top of techno music and laughter in the background. Aaron could almost make out the telltale snort of Delia's laughter that usually took place at his expense. "Delia's here with some friends. She just showed up a few minutes ago."

"Did she say anything about me?" Aaron's hope flared.

His first serious girlfriend, Delia had turned his simple existence upside down with the infamous words spoken in her usual flippant manner, "I think we should see other people." This wonderful news was followed by the even more infamous relationship killer, "But we can still be friends!" It had been a very long and humbling week since her mercilessly delivered one-two combo knocked him for a loop.

Kyle paused, his silence implied things better left unsaid. "She's playing it off like everything's totally cool. Honestly, she looks happy to be single."

Aaron blew out the breath he'd been holding in.

Kyle reassured, "Don't worry about it, there's plenty of fish in the sea." Kyle's casual manner didn't translate. Aaron had never found it simple to catch either fish or women.

He prepared himself for another pep talk. Kyle had been pushing him for the last week to broaden his horizons and do exactly as Delia suggested— *see other people.* He'd told Aaron repeatedly he'd be better off with someone else. Kyle didn't care much for Delia's manipulations.

"Look, I know you're stuck on her, but you're not getting anywhere by chasing her. The best way to handle a girl like Delia is to hook up with her friends. If that doesn't drive her batshit crazy, then she doesn't deserve you." Sage advice from philosopher Kyle.

2

"Do you think she told everyone we broke up?" Aaron feared he already knew the answer.

"You mean that she kicked you to the curb? Yeah dude. That boat has sailed, there ain't no stopping it. That's why you gotta make some moves of your own. Offense dude, time for offense. You remember that chica Delia's always hangin' with, the sexy one with black hair, Amber?"

"Ahh … yeah, I think so."

"She's here right now, so hurry up, her tight little ass is ripe. And hey … um … can you pick up some beer on the way home? You know how it goes. You get a few drinks in em' and the pants fall right off."

Only if you're Kyle. Aaron had never experienced the good fortune of having women's pants fall off. His limited intimate encounters taught him there was considerable effort and occasional begging involved in the removal of women's clothing.

"Yeah, I caught some decent tips tonight. How about a twelve pack?" He already knew the answer, but to ask was habitual, an endless game he and Kyle played. Kyle never wanted less beer. Kyle always pushed for more, and he always had a plausible reason.

"Better make it a case. I think we're in for an all-nighter."

"Alright, I guess I'll get a case, just in case we need a case." The cheesy punch line had ceased being funny months ago. But like most aspects of Aaron's life, it had become a groove he'd fallen into that he couldn't get out of. He hung up and headed out the front door of Bemichis into the New York streets to do the same thing he did night after night.

Kyle had called for the beer. The moral support play wasn't his thing. In fact, Kyle was probably making moves on Amber at that very moment. Aaron didn't mind. Kyle had a few redeeming qualities worthy of mention. Loyalty, yes, loyalty would be one, that and a never ending supply of optimism. The proverbial glass was always half full with Kyle—*half full of beer.*

But Aaron didn't make it home this night. He never made it to the corner drug store for beer. The moment he exited Bemichis, fate conspired to place two opposing and dangerous forces in his path; the timing so impeccably perfect, one could argue divine intervention.

The first party, a vision so remarkable, so drop dead gorgeous, she seemed surreal against the backdrop of grainy darkness and gloom of the concrete-asphalt streets. Aaron's world blurred out of focus. This sparkling gem of a five-foot blonde-bomb package complete with cliché black cocktail dress and *fuck me* pumps was the only thing to remain distinct in his vision. As she locked an unblinking gaze on him, nothing else existed in his universe. Nothing mattered beyond this fabulous woman gliding towards him with supreme grace and poise.

3

As he was drawn to the blonde's powerful magnetic attraction, the second part of the equation arrived on scene. Aaron watched in fascination as an unmarked police cruiser drew up alongside her. He recognized the undercover cop car by the telltale spotlight next to the driver-side mirror.

The woman hesitated, appearing torn between giving her attention to Aaron or them. She was so far out of his league. Why did she notice him at all?

The men in the car beckoned to her. Her hesitation ended, she turned away to converse with the undercovers. She probably didn't know they were cops. The one on the passenger side propositioned her, "Hey babe, what's goin' on tonight?"

Without missing a beat, she offered, "*Monsieur* would like to party? *Un ménage à trois?* We can make a party, *oui?*" She had an intoxicating French accent.

Both cops hopped out of the car instantly, surrounding her in an unmistakably threatening stance. Aaron advanced on the trio to better hear them. He couldn't take his eyes off the woman to save his life.

The fat, bulldog cop verbally assaulted her in his Brooklyn accent. "Hey, who you workin' for? I hope it's somebody we know. You gotta be paid up with the right people to work this street!"

She frowned. "I don't work for anyone!"

Aaron was further smitten as he watched her defy them in her cute little French accent. The bulldog grabbed her arm, "You're under arrest!"

The thin, bald, Barney Fife-looking cop, moved in to grab her other arm. They must think she's a prostitute. How could they make such a mistake?

* * * *

She studied the two fools, one on each arm. She examined their auras and evaluated her options. Their auras swirled with the colors of arrogance and a sense of entitlement. Like so many others who came before them, these men craved power over her. It was a base instinct to control and possess, as if they had found a new toy to play with. Their selfish desires disgusted her, like a rotten stench surrounding something putrid. She read the nuances of their hatred towards all women stemming from a sense of inadequacy. Their souls held a deeply rooted taint from a lifetime of police corruption fueled by greed.

They were a prime example of what was wrong with the world today, authority figures seeking out the seemingly weak for predatory purposes. Nothing new. She'd been dealing with the sick desires of small-minded men for a very long time. She couldn't help but shiver with disgust and loathing, an involuntary reaction to something so unpleasant.

Glancing at the handsome boy, she immediately noticed the severe contrast between the foul detectives and the purity of spirit evidenced in the colors of his aura. By comparison he appeared a saint, worthy of canonization in his child-like innocence.

His overt infatuation and innocence called to her, she found it hard to resist. She wished she'd followed her initial impulse to ignore the detectives when they stopped their car. She should have focused on this adorable young man who was so taken with her. As she watched the colors of his aura shift, she perceived his indignant response to the detectives man-handling her. A window of opportunity opened up.

* * * *

Aaron burned, outraged at the audacity of the grotesque, bulldog of a man assaulting the blonde goddess. An involuntary cry tore from his throat, "Hey! Leave her alone! Get your hands off her!" He couldn't believe either of these crude creatures would dare lay hands on the beautiful vision of perfection who spoke in an intoxicating stream of French obscenities.

"T'as une tête à faire soutier les plaques d'égouts!" She blasted the bulldog. Aaron recalled just enough French to know she'd told him his face could blow off manhole covers. *"Cessez de me cracher dessus pendant que vous par lez"* Wiping her face, she eloquently expressed her disgust that the bulldog was spitting on her as he spoke.

Never ceasing her tirade of lovely French filth, the blonde struck in a blur. In one swift move, she broke the bulldog's hold on her wrist and clawed his face. A trail of bloody slash marks opened across his left cheek. Without pause she pivoted and punched Barney Fife in the nose with a gratifying crunch. His head snapped backwards and a splat of blood flew through the air. She pivoted in a split-second to face the bulldog, a Taser in hand. She had magically snatched the weapon from Barney Fife after breaking his nose.

The combat unfolded before Aaron's eyes like a scene from a martial arts film. The woman appeared to move in a blur, with superhuman velocity. By comparison to her whip-like actions, the cops creeped along in slow motion.

Aaron's jaw dropped in complete awe. He had difficulty accepting these bizarre events for reality. As the shimmery cocktail-dressed wonder woman fired her stolen Taser, Aaron recognized the bulldog wasn't really as slow as he had seemed. He had a pistol drawn and moving upward in a sweeping arc.

THE NIGHTLIFE NEW YORK

Aaron's dream state shattered along with his heretofore unremarkable and short life when the Taser struck the bulldog at precisely the moment his gun sights aligned with Aaron. The electric shock of the Taser began a domino effect. All muscles and tendons in the bulldog's body clenched, including his trigger finger. The sharp crack of the gun blasted a slug straight through Aaron's chest, knocking him to the ground with the impact.

The pain came seconds later, delayed. It hit in an all-consuming, overpowering rush. Nothing existed beyond the horrible agony of his chest torn to shreds by the wicked projectile. He wasn't brave or manly or noble like all these scenes of bullet wounds in Hollywood films. He screamed and howled in pain, and promptly blacked out.

* * * *

SMACK, SMACK, SMACK. A cool, soft palm hit Aaron's face three times. He opened his eyes to an angel, a halo of light around her tousled, golden curls like the corona encircling the sun. She had the most succulent puffy lips and a benevolent shine of concern and compassion.

"Are you an angel?" His beautiful seraph began swearing up a storm in melodic French.

"*Le réalité' et toi vous ne vous entendez pas, n'est-ce pas?*" She remarked on his disconnect with reality.

He didn't know what to say. How do you greet the angel of death?

"*C'est vraiment des conneries!*" The words seeped in slowly, sparking a memory from French class—*this is bullshit.* Are angels supposed to curse?

The heavy weight of exhaustion settled in with a cold numbness. *Is this what it feels like to die?* He drifted back into unconsciousness, content in the belief that heavenly hosts carried him off to a better place.

* * * *

CHAPTER 2

She knew she couldn't stay on the street. The detectives would not remain incapacitated much longer and the gun shot would probably bring a 911 call from the restaurant down the block. The unfortunate boy who foolishly tried to intervene on her behalf was bleeding to death. A decision had to be made. She felt guilty, responsible for what happened to him. If she had paid closer attention she'd have disarmed the fat, idiot cop before hitting him with the Taser.

"Je suis ici pour toi. I am here for you." She tried to comfort the young man in his pain and delirium. Living most of her life in Paris, she tended to backslide into her native tongue in moments of high stress.

"Je vais le regretter." Knowing she would probably regret it, she made the snap decision to take responsibility for him. Without another second's delay she scooped him up in her arms, cradling him like a child. He weighed about 165 lbs., nothing for her preternaturally strong physique. Though only 110 lbs., she could easily lift several times her own body weight.

She sped down the street, away from the restaurant and the blood-splattered sidewalk. She opted for the dark alleys, keeping out of sight as she ran flat out with the young man in her arms and her Prada heels hanging by the straps in her teeth. It was damn near impossible to run in high heels.

She reached her fourth floor apartment via the fire escape catwalk and took stock of the situation. He'd lost too much blood already and was losing more every second. She had to stop the bleeding, now. He smelled delicious, wonderful red syrup all over his shirt, and the scent raw meat. She could barely stand to be near him without feeding. Her sharp teeth came out full length, ready to sink into all that juicy flesh. She swallowed down her urges and forced herself to lean in close. Her mouth filled with venom like a dog salivating over a meal held under its nose. Might be helpful. The boy need the healing and pain-killing properties of her venom.

Forcing herself not to bite, she licked away the blood and gore to reveal his lean, well-toned chest. He had long striated musculature from work and everyday use—no iron-pumped, steroid-induced, weightlifter bulges. Not an ounce of fat on his young, sleek torso. His high cheek bones and angular features lent him a sharp, elfin look. He had light skin with dark hair and eyes, reminiscent of a Spaniard or Italian. *Il est très bea. Oui, he is very fine. The gaping wound does spoil it.*

The boy's bleeding slowed, but didn't stop entirely. Somehow he managed to gain consciousness for a few moments. His lazy eyes looked up at her, glazed and drugged. Her venom had worked its chemical magic of pain-killer-endorphin-dump. But it was not enough. A more drastic remedy would be necessary. She noticed the change in his aura, and smelled his impending death from shock and trauma. Her first aid could only delay the inevitable and perhaps make his demise relatively painless.

The only way she could see to reverse his fate was to give him her life blood, making him as she was. She hated to do it, had purposely avoided it for many years. If he survived the change, it would create an unbreakable psychic bond, bending his will to hers. She would be his master, and he enslaved—not a convenient arrangement for either party.

She knew how it felt to be enthralled and enslaved by such a bond to a master. She had hated every single minute of it. The irresistible imprint had forced her to submit to her former master's every command, her body and mind acting according to his will.

She vowed years ago to never subject another person to the humiliation of enslavement that she had endured. Granted, she didn't believe herself to be sadistic or intentionally malicious. Until now, she had never been willing to do this with anyone. If she was to try, it shouldn't be without his consent. That's how it had been with her, forced, with no knowledge of what was happening at the time. At the very least she should give him a choice before going forward.

"What is your name?" He smiled up at her as she licked his blood from her lips.

"Aaron." A huge stupid grin slid across his face.

"Aaron, you must listen carefully. I cannot stop the bleeding. Your wound is very serious. Is something I can do for you. But you must understand first. If I do this, you will be bound to me always. If I give you this lifesaving gift you must serve me in all things. Your life will belong to me. Do you understand?"

"Yeah." The strong pain-killer of her venom had obviously done its job. That goofy grin of his just wouldn't quit. "You must be an angel. Keep talking, I love the sound of your voice."

"I do this, it cannot be reversed. Is very important you understand."

He licked his dry lips. "I need a drink. I am so thirsty."

"*Oui*, in a moment, but do you comprehend?"

"Yes, it's okay. Do what you have to, but I'd like a drink now." His eyes rolled shut. He was slipping away.

A quick flick of her nails across her wrist opened a lifeline for him. With his permission, she gave him a drink. He almost gagged at his first taste as she rubbed her wrist over his lips, but this urge was quickly overcome as he continued to lick at her. Soon his lips sucked from her skin with a will of their own, like an infant's involuntary reaction to a mother's nipple placed in his mouth.

Greedy for more, he grabbed her arm and gripped her tight, sucking harder. After a moment, she decided he'd had enough. She couldn't afford for him to weaken her too much. She pried her arm from his two-handed grip with a yank and a wet sound as she broke his suction from her wrist.

It was done and could not be undone.

* * * *

Drifting through a hazy blend of pain and drugged happiness, he felt his body begin to tingle all over. The slight tickle-tingling sensation gradually changed intensity to an ache. The ache began to throb, coming on in waves, and then became a constant pain. The pain morphed to a burning sensation, which became an all-consuming inferno raging through his body. He kicked and thrashed. He cried out in agony as flaming trails of molten fire blazed across his flesh.

He fainted repeatedly from the intense scorching pain, only to awake to more agony. He welcomed the periods of unconsciousness, the pain receding as he sank into oblivion. Eventually he reached such a point of exhaustion and fatigue that the pain no longer woke him.

In the midst of his delirium of pain he dreamt. He dreamed of Delia. She smiled invitingly, slipping her hands over his arms and chest with soft little strokes. A Delia far nicer and sweeter than she'd ever been before. Then her features changed to a vicious scowl, mocking him with words of rejection and taunts. A little closer to the Delia he knew, though a bit harsher. Her cute little half smile alternated back and forth to a sneer. At one point she even swung at him, cursing him for leaving her behind as he moved on to somewhere else ... somewhere different where she couldn't follow. These nightmarish dreams replayed repeatedly. Over and over, more of the same theme, Delia invited him in with seductive attentions, and then turned on him viciously as they became intimate.

On occasion his mother appeared asking *what are you doing? Are you ever planning on going to college?* Strange to see her there. She rarely ever called and virtually never stopped by his apartment, so why should she be in his dreams? The one person he needed to see most never showed up, he'd been gone for six years. Aaron stopped dreaming of his father years ago.

At some point in his delirium, the dream sequence changed. He became angry, violent. He seized ahold of Delia with great strength and shook her bodily like a rag doll. She laughed as though it was nothing.

Then his guardian angel arrived. The blond angel's smile radiated a sense of calm. With her touch, he stilled instantly, all concerns erased by her charisma. She soothed him, taking away the aggression, and removing Delia from his nightmares.

The tenor of his dreams shifted. It turned into a tour, a ride through a video game. He became a passenger in someone else's world. A strangely exhilarating experience in a strange city where the people spoke in foreign languages. He dreamed of racing through the night, moving at unbelievable speeds through the streets. It was like living in someone else's body while he ran at the velocity of a motorbike with nothing but his own two feet to propel him.

His guardian angel came and went repeatedly. She helped cool his burning fever with a wet washcloth, but her eyes and her touch brought the most comfort. She fed him warm broth from a cup. It tasted wonderful. He wanted more to quench his thirst. It seemed he could never get enough of her broth. She shushed him and assured that *all is well* in her sensual French accent, but she denied him more drink—*not too much, mon cher*. His angel held him cradled in her arms like a baby. At times the fever and pain, so intense, he knew he'd died and gone to Hell, burning in the eternal lake of fire. She held him even when he felt so hot his skin would surely burn her from the incredible heat.

Always the visions of Delia returned, laughing, mocking him, until his angel arrived to chase her away. He'd been banished to a special level of Hell, tormented endlessly by demonic versions of Delia.

Sometime later, maybe days, or perhaps even weeks, the Delia attacks ceased. His life had been claimed by the angel. She fought off his demons and took a permanent position as his guardian. Delia no longer held sway. But the dreams became more disturbing, visions of stalking through the dark alleys at night. He moved swift and sure, attacking his prey ferociously. He fed from their necks, drinking blood by the gallons—from hundreds of faces of men and women in all parts of the world, all colors and races. No matter how much blood he drank it could never be enough. His horrible thirst could never be sated.

* * * *

CHAPTER 3

Michelle had never done this before. She wasn't even certain it would work. Her own transformation hadn't been accompanied by an instruction manual. Many aspects of her life had been learned the hard way, through painful mistakes and experimentation. Her former master hadn't been very forthcoming. The bastard had no regard for her or anyone else.

She watched Aaron as he thrashed and squirmed, tossing the covers from his feverish body. Seeing this trim, fit, well-endowed young man in her bed inspired a mess of conflicting emotions. A flush of arousal warmed her as she slid her hand over him, feeling his hot feverish skin. His face pinched in anguish, and she wished there was more she could do beyond a soothing word and a cool, wet cloth. Her touch seemed to calm him. He kept complaining of thirst, so she fed him a little more blood, but not too much. She beefed up her own feeding schedule to accommodate Aaron's demands.

As time stretched into the third night, and his fever hadn't subsided, she began to think that perhaps he wouldn't make it. *What a shame, such a lovely boy.* She considered it might be more humane to kill him now, put him out of his pain and misery. She wasn't sure how long the process should take, it seemed like it should be a couple days, but who knew? Perhaps it was different with each person.

She kicked herself for doing it. Surely a mistake, she should have let him die. What would she do with him if he did come out of it? She had lived alone for decades. She wasn't exactly prepared to share her life with anyone. What a foolish, impetuous thing to do. She should end it now, save both of them from years of complications.

She put her hands around his neck. It would be so easy, one flick of her wrist, spinal column severed. He opened his eyes delirious with fever. For a moment he looked at her, recognized her, and his expression morphed to relief. He mumbled something about *my angel.* The fool was hallucinating. He smiled at her with adoration and undisguised worship. That did it. She couldn't go through with the dirty deed. It wasn't in her to be so cruel. It would have to wait until he provoked her. Then she could get past his damnable boyish charm.

What would it be like to share her life with someone? It had been a very long time since she'd let anyone get so close and personal. She'd tried to have relationships with a few men before—what a disaster. A painful lesson she had learned repeatedly—she didn't mix well with people, at least not for any length of time. Those experiments always ended in death. No matter what she did, no matter how hard she tried, men always died. They were so frail, their bodies so easily broken, withered by time and sickness, by her need for blood. A sure recipe for heartache.

But this would be different. This man would be subject to her command. He wouldn't be able to beat and abuse her like her master did. The kid better watch himself. If he became a problem, she knew how to handle it, but he'd get his chance.

She reached back through the years to remember her life long ago with a male vampire. Those memories were too dark, filled with violence and malice. Her former master had been quite the sadist. But there were some passionate moments of wicked pleasure. She remembered how they molded together in painful, savage sexual adventures. He dominated her like no other, so strong, so vicious, and she had enjoyed it immensely. And the synchronous bites! Those wonderful sensations of blood, sex and venom all rolled into one insane, chaotic blend. There was nothing like it.

Aaron would have his chance. She'd be gentle with him at first. He was definitely an innocent. This time she would dominate, the boy would answer to her in all things. But if he began to exhibit the signs, if he became anything like her former master, she'd snap his neck without a moment's hesitation.

* * * *

Aaron awoke to a bone dry thirst and a dull throbbing ache in his chest. He heard a myriad of sounds ranging from snores and grunts to dishwashing and several televisions blasting over one another. He breathed in crisp, strong smells of linen, cotton, vinyl, paint, a woman's perfume, carpet freshener, and lemon furniture polish. Each scent had its own distinct signature. He differentiated them with amazing clarity.

"Where the hell am I?"

Bemichis. He had just left work, then the blonde and cops. And he'd been shot! He reached up to feel his chest.

"Holy shit!"

Nothing, not a mark on him. The gunshot wound had completely healed, although he seemed to have some residual soreness. That's when he noticed he was completely naked under the bed covers. Though the bedroom was dark, he could see clearly. It seemed the room had light, but from where?

12

Definitely not his room or his apartment. This place had a feminine touch, the bedspreads, furniture, candles. A woman's home. And the perfume scent evoked a sense of something vaguely familiar—cloudy, dream-like memories of being soothed and comforted by a French-speaking angel with a heavenly smile and golden hair.

Nothing made sense. He should be dead, or in some kind of coma or intensive care unit. Yet he felt great

He listened to noises coming from outside this room, but not just from the other room. *Were those sounds from the neighboring apartments?* The walls must be ultra-thin. The sounds came to him as though they were people standing in the room right beside him.

Something waited at the edge of his perceptions, some sense of another person, a woman in the other room. She was coming to him, coming towards the door to the room. He felt an indefinable attraction to her. She opened the bedroom door, her golden hair illuminated from behind by the living room light spilling through into the room. His guardian angel.

He recalled how she held him, wiped his brow, tenderly ministered to him. She had somehow healed him, brought him out of the bowels of Hell.

He recognized the magnetic pull effect he felt was to her, like an invisible line connecting them. Michelle. Her name was Michelle, but he couldn't recall how he knew it. She had come for him, and she had many things to explain. And how did he know that?

* * * *

Michelle studied him for a second, taking in the small details, the nuances of change. Aaron's aura held an animal magnetism that had not existed prior to his change. Much more attractive, somehow manlier. She wanted to sink her fangs into him and experience sex with one of her own kind again.

She had grown so accustomed to these fragile and delicate human men. Like a carnivore forced to subsist on a vegetarian diet, she hungered for some meat. She needed a real man, a strong, virile vampire.

She restrained her carnal urges for the moment. Plenty of time for fun later. And she didn't want to scare her new companion. He should be brought into the fold gently. Though he had come through the change, his aura still displayed an innocent soul. She sighed. She expected that the inner beast, the vampire's true nature, would rear its ugly head soon enough. Until then, she'd handle him with kid gloves.

* * * *

13

"Bonjour, how does it feel to be reborn?" She smiled slyly.

"I could down a gallon of water right now. Beyond that, I'm good, all things considered." He tried for nonchalant, but felt childish and unsophisticated in her presence. He suspected she wasn't an angel after all. He caught a sense, a feeling, that she was quite mischievous and not necessarily benign. He recalled a vague memory of extreme burning pain, but it seemed as though it had all been a weird dream. How could he have been in so much pain and yet sit here in this bed, in good health, not a mark on him? His mind raced as she slowly advanced towards the bed, staring intently. Confused, clueless, he remained silent.

"Many things, they change for you now. You have noticed you can hear all the petit noises, *n'est pas?* You can smell and taste everything, *non?* Your senses are very acute?"

"Ahmm ... yeah, I guess"

"Listen and I will explain." She sat on the edge of the bed next to him. Her gaze held his, never blinking even once. Creepy.

He finally had a chance to take a good close look at her. Michelle was far more attractive than he first thought. Her eyes held a vibrant shade of green he'd never seen before. Her round face was pleasingly symmetrical with a narrow, elegant neck sweeping up to her cheeks. Graceful, very patrician. She had creamy-white perfect skin, a light, pink blush to her cheeks. Too perfect. She could have been an airbrushed artist's rendering, unnaturally beautiful. The smirk on her face led him to believe she knew exactly what was on his mind.

"Is difficult, we are strangers. But you must believe what I say is the truth. Do you trust me, Aaron?"

"I'm pretty sure you saved my life, why shouldn't I trust you?" he replied with false bravado. Who was she? Why did she bring him to her apartment? Her words started to freak him out.

She nodded. "I did something I promised to never do. I gave you new life. Is like a special kind of virus. This allows for miraculous regeneration and healing. There are changes you will notice, you are very different now." She sounded so sexy purring biological terminologies with her poetic accent. He didn't have the first clue what she was saying, sounded like sci-fi mumbo jumbo.

"Your body now needs regular infusions of fresh blood. Is the only nourishment you require. You will not consume food or drink, only fresh blood. You noticed the thirst is intense, *oui?"*

He didn't know what to make of her. He stared at her with a raised eyebrow. *Are you for real? Are you properly medicated?*

She continued, "*Arriver au point*, you are now a vampire, and you must feed on fresh blood very soon." Her cute accent now held the potential to become irritating. He shook his head no, an involuntary reaction to the overpowering denial resounding through his mind like a pounding drum beating out a steady rhythm of *No! No! No! No!* This had to be some kind of sick joke. At any moment, people would fill the room with cameras and smiles yelling, "Hey dude, you've been punked!"

She didn't give him much time to react. "I can see you do not believe me. *Donc*, I will demonstrate!"

With a flick of her hand she sliced her wicked nails her left wrist and held it a couple inches from his face. The wondrous smell of sweet, delicious blood assaulted his senses. His mouth watered at the strong, savory perfume pulling him down to lick from her wrist. Like a shark drawn to the scent of blood in the water, he couldn't resist its lure. His mind reeled in revulsion, but his thirst overwhelmed him. He latched onto her wrist with a snake-like chomp, sucking frantically. *Awesome.* He couldn't resist, and he was *sooo* thirsty. He bit down hard into her open wound, his sharp little canines punctured through her flesh like biting into a juicy peach. *Oh God, that's wonderful, more, more, MORE!* He devoured every drop of the succulent syrup. He had never tasted anything like it. He didn't think he could ever stop. He wanted to drain her arm, wring it dry like a sponge.

Michelle moaned. Her breathing quickened, she panted heavily like a dog and her legs squirmed. "*Oui! Oui!*" Small gasps of intense pleasure spilled from her lips. Suddenly she sat back and in a deep, resonating timbre of voice commanded, "Enough! *Ça suffit!*"

Reacting instantly to her command, he released his lockjaw hold on her wrist. The truth hit him like a bucket of ice-water, drenching him with shock. He had just fed from her slashed wrist like some bloodthirsty animal. He reeled and pitched, losing equilibrium. He leaned back against the pillow of the bed as his head spun. He couldn't believe it, wouldn't believe. He tried to deny the delicious smell of blood in his nostrils and the gut-gnawing hunger for *more*. He tried to plug his nose, to think of anything other than the blood.

He couldn't deny what he'd just done. He had to face the irrefutable facts. He enjoyed her blood immensely. It was the most wonderful sensation, almost better than sex. He understood without a shadow of doubt that he needed blood. He'd do anything to get it, like a junky jonesin' for a fix, like a fish needs water to breath. He had the blood *smores*, and he needed *more*. The burning, itchy, dry throat was bad, but to top it off he had a *hunger*, a potent *need*.

Michelle twitched and made little groaning sounds, still pulsing with her response to his bite. She watched him with a half-lidded, lazy-eyed look, as though drugged. "Mmm … *oh la vache!* Ooh … I like that very much." She paused to regain her composure. She retained the lazy *Garfield-the-cat* half-lidded smile.

"There are details I must explain first and then we will see to our needs properly." She wiped a hand across her face. "When you were dying from the gunshot, I fed you the same way, from my blood. This has brought on the change. You are now like me, but also *tied* to me. This is a very special connection. You are blood of my blood and you will answer to me when I command." Michelle paused for a moment then continued, holding his gaze with a look of apology in her eyes.

"I am sorry you must live this way. Is the only way to save your life. Your injuries were too severe." Her eyes seemed to beg his forgiveness for what she had done. "Now you must consume one liter fresh blood every night until you learn to control the thirst. I will teach you how we live. Is relatively simple. There are many benefits and pleasures. The most obvious; you age very slowly, like dog years in reverse. Fifty years is like one year to you." She smiled at him hopefully.

Shocked by his ravenous consumption of her blood, the implications of her words seeped in slowly. He sat there dazed and confused, wishing people would jump out of the closet and tell him this was all a gag.

She continued. "You are now very strong, many times stronger than before. And you can move much faster than *people*. They will be turtles, moving in slow motion. You are not immortal. You can die, but is very difficult. Your body is resilient, you heal rapidly."

He was at a loss for words. He stared at her silently, and then glanced at the closet, hoping.

"You and I have a very special bond that cannot be broken. You will know things about me. I can send to you. You are sending to me. Is like telepathy. *Oui?* You understand? *Comprends?*" He simply nodded his head in silent acquiescence.

She went on. "I will teach you to close your mind. Is like a radio station to me. I can hear the station all the time." That got his attention.

He popped up from his dazed stupor. "You mean you're hearing my thoughts right now?"

She smiled reassuringly. "*Oui, reste calme,* my silly American boy. This is no *problème*. As I told you, we have a special connection. I will show you how to remain private in here." She tapped on her head and smiled again.

He returned her smile with embarrassment. He caught the distinct impression she approved of him. He had no cause for shame or concern. The truth of it staggered him. *She's in my head! Oh. My. God. She's in my fuckin' head!*

Her smile let him know that she understood. It was okay. But it wasn't okay! Nothing would ever be okay again! This beautiful, callous, psychotic, foreign woman had invaded his mind, sending him messages and reading his thoughts. *What a mindfuck! This is really happening!*

"You must remember I am now your master. When I command, you will obey. There is no choice. Also, is very important, we live the nightlife, after dark. No sunlight. We are extremely sensitive to the sun. You will burn very badly in the sun. We sleep in the day."

"No!" He grabbed his head. "No! This is too much. It's too fast." He shook his head trying to dislodge the horrifying thoughts pelting through his consciousness. "This is too weird!"

Lucky for him, she understood how he felt. "Don't worry. I am not some evil creature. I will not abuse my authority over you. You must trust me. You have no choice. *C'est la vie!*" She shrugged her shoulders in a flippant *such is life* manner.

"As soon as you tell me where my clothes are, I'm gone. You got a great scam goin' here, but I'm not buying it." He had trouble getting past the feeling this was all some kind of cruel joke.

He looked around the room for any sign of his clothes. Michelle reached out to put her hand in his. Instantly it was there, that sense of *rightness*, a feeling everything would be *okay*, because she was there, she had it all figured out. He wondered if she was manipulating his emotions through this weird connection. Then he noticed her unblemished wrist. No marks at all from having been slashed open just minutes before. Not a cut or scab.

That was it.

He had enough Twilight Zone horseshit for one night. "You're screwing with my head! What kinda drugs did you give me?" He let go her hand and jabbed a finger of accusation at her flawlessly healed skin. "That is so not right! I saw you cut yourself!"

He was reaching the edge, staring into the abyss of madness, where reality and insanity blend together in an inseparable concoction that leaves men babbling in the street. He was about to lose it.

"*Oui.* This is the way of things with our kind. One of the many benefits of this life."

Michelle stood up abruptly. "Put your clothes on. I will show you, our life is very simple." He blanched.

He was naked beneath the covers. He must have been naked when she was doing whatever she did to him. She smiled and patted his hand in a motherly fashion.

"You Americans are so silly with your modesty. Don't worry. I have not done anything with your body. Not yet!" With that she walked out of the room smirking and closed the door behind her. He instantly knew there were clothes for him in the top drawer of the dresser. He knew like he had known her name without a single word spoken. *She's in my fucking head again! Oh. My. God!*

* * * *

CHAPTER 4

They began sitting cross-legged, face to face. Aaron couldn't think of anything but Michelle. She wore a slip of a white dress, very short, nothing more than a nightie. As she sat there, legs splayed wide, he appreciated every detail and contour of her inner thighs and skimpy white underwear. Utterly impossible to concentrate on anything she said.

"Please close your eyes!" she snapped at him with a knowing smirk on her face. "Picture me in your mind."

Easy.

Sitting there, the curves of her breasts and thighs calling to him, her devious little smile promised sex—lots of sex. Gradually his mind's eye view of her changed. Not that the picture was different per se, but now he sensed something more. This beautiful hundred pound kitten exuded a power, a force of personality like a massive lioness. He caught her amusement. Not mocking him, it was more the pleasure one derives from watching a child walk for the first time.

He knew she viewed him as child-like, and this test of their connectivity was the equivalent of baby steps. He hoped he didn't botch it. He didn't want to make a fool of himself.

He concentrated further on the woman who was really a lioness in human skin, and delved into her psyche. He sensed her attraction to him, her desire to both fuck and bite him at the same time. In the middle of this desire was a vague memory of another time, a very far away time. Shadows of another man, but not exactly a man. The shadows mixed together in a blend of longing, desire, and hatred. There was a sense of violence, extreme violence, and sex.

Suddenly his mind slammed into a blank wall. He could perceive no emotion, no thought, only the image of Michelle accompanied by her powerful predatory nature held tightly under her iron control. He wondered what would happened if she lost control.

He heard her voice, but not with his ears. The sensation was so much more, replete with intent, an irresistible force of command. {{Imagine yourself, your mind, sealed within a steel box. Is like a vault. Picture your mind enclosed within a vault.}}

He did as she instructed, and instantly recognized a closure, a blocked layer of protection closing his mind off from the world around him.

{{Very good. Is easy for you.}} She spoke again directly in his mind, and he registered her approval and relief at his ability to do this the first time, without difficulty.

It occurred to him that if he was blocked, how could he still hear her in his mind? Why wasn't she blocked out? A sick feeling hit his gut as he began to suspect that maybe he could not attain any privacy. Would he be doomed to a life where his every thought, no matter how petty and disgusting, his every sin was laid bare for her perusal? Who could live with such a burden? Could any man live every moment of every day with perfect thoughts? He worked himself into a panic. In his distress, his neat little mental vault failed completely.

"Michelle, how can I still hear you if I'm inside my vault?"

"Aaron, *ne t'inquiet pas*, you were closed to me, your mind blocked."

He interrupted, "But ..."

She spoke over the top of him. "But I can send to you. Don't worry. Is always this way. I can send to you always. You can send to me always." She sent him a calm feeling, letting him know she approved of him without reservation. He felt that same sense that everything was gonna be *okay*. It seemed to help. He relaxed and gradually became embarrassed over his panic attack.

She spoke again into his mind. {{Try to reach me and read my thoughts. You will see how it is when we are blocked. You cannot read me when I choose to be private. Is the same with you.}}

He strained so hard, he found himself physically leaning towards her as he flowed down through their connection. He hit a solid blank wall where her mind should have been. Nothing. Not a damn thing. He couldn't read one nuance of meaning from her apart from the fact she sat there smirking at him, pleased. He continued to hit her blank wall, and so he pushed harder, concentrating on reaching with all his intensity. His mind washed over and around Michelle, engulfing her, but not finding a way in. He kept reaching out until he sensed others in the surrounding residences. Aaron touched on an older man, someone in his sixties whose mind was hazy with alcohol from the six pack of Bud Light he drank while camped in front of the TV. The old man's mind was filled with speculations of football statistics and possible outcomes for the game.

As soon as Aaron noticed the man's mind, he also became aware of the woman who slept in the bedroom of the same apartment a few yards away. Her mind was deeply shrouded in dreams, a cloudy world of images and feelings, something about her sister and her husband, the man watching football. She dreamt of the vague details of an illicit affair between her husband and her younger, more attractive, sister.

The woman's emotions were in turmoil over the dream, a frenzied mix of anger, resentment, jealousy, and self-loathing for her inability to retain her husband's attention and affections. She writhed in anxiety, fighting with her own sheets and blankets.

Aaron had enough of this and reached out in other directions, seeking what else he might encounter. Completely absorbed in his psychic scanning, he had lost focus on Michelle and his internal privacy block.

He touched on a teenage girl who chatted online with her boyfriend. She was typing frantically on her laptop, trying to justify her actions to her boyfriend. She had gone to a party with one of her girlfriends, drank too much, and ended up in the bedroom with another guy. She didn't want her boyfriend to know how far things had actually gone.

Michelle snatched his attention away from his psionic ramblings with a psychic push. Her mind shoved his mind, a very disorientating experience. He grabbed for something, reaching out with his hands to stabilize himself on the carpet. He felt off balance, dizzy, but she hadn't touched him physically at all.

In the moment of her psychic *push*, Michelle transmitted flashes of surprise, anger, and envy for a split second before slipping back behind the blank wall of her vault. He remembered himself and refocused on his own mental vault, reestablishing his privacy.

She stood up abruptly. "You were reading their minds, *oui?*" She gave him a raised eyebrow, looking down on him. "You are better at this game than I thought. Enough practice for tonight."

He realized he had transmitted his encounters with the neighbors directly to her. He was would have to learn to multitask, to maintain his mental vault while scanning others nearby. He suspected it might be like trying to chew gum, pat your head, and rub your belly all at once. Not impossible, but tricky.

"Why didn't you tell me I could do that?"

Her irritation leaked through their emotional ties, her eyes flashed in anger. "I did not ..."

"You didn't know?" He spoke over the top of her when he realized the truth. His ability was unique.

"*Non*," she snapped curtly.

He swelled with pride, a childish feeling of superiority and wonder at this magnificent new existence. He speculated about what new experiences, as yet undiscovered, this life might hold for him.

"I see the auras, but I cannot read minds apart from yours." She flashed her eyes again, a demand for submission. He knew she was testing to see if he would take the bait and rise up, only to be slapped down. He wasn't adversarial or proud, nor foolish enough to be baited into a challenge. He looked down away from her in the universal sign of submission. He stayed seated while she stared down on him, standing over him like a master ready to whip her slave for taking undue liberties.

After a moment of glaring without catching a rise out of him, Michelle softened. "You have every right to be intrigued. *Pourquoi est-ce que je dois être celui avec le gamin spécial?*"

He barely understood her. She had said something about being stuck with the special boy. *Special like the kids on the short bus.*

She reached out her hand to pull him up. "The aura tells me of moods and personalities. I knew things from your aura the night we met. I knew those men were *police corrompue*, and they would create *beaucoup de problèmes*, but I did not know they would shoot you. I cannot read minds, or see the future." She admitted this apologetically as he stood up to face her.

"No more conflict." With this she returned to the role of benevolent master she had assumed upon his awakening. Michelle placed her hands on his head, holding him straight, directing his eyes into her gaze. She restarted her instruction with the basics of mesmerizing people through direct eye contact and subtle commands.

"It is *magnétisme animal.* Is natural we attract the prey. We are predators." She stared unblinking, drawing him in with those entrancing vivid green eyes. He felt her looking down into his soul. She owned him with nothing more than her gaze. She broke the eye contact, yet again leaving him with a feeling of child-like inadequacy.

She spoke reassuringly, "You will see tonight. Women will come to you all the time. They are easy prey." She spoke as though it was a normal, everyday thing to hunt people like animals in the wild.

"When feeding, there is a chemical, *une médicament puissant.* Is like strong drugs." She opened her mouth inhumanly wide. Her jaw unhinged like some kind of beast that would swallow him whole. She pointed at her elongated canines tapering to razor sharp little points. He took a step back out of her reach, fear and morbid fascination dueling to keep him in place.

"You mean like the venom of a snake?" He sputtered nervously.

She snapped her mouth shut as if it had never happened. "*Exactement.* This *médicament* heals the bite marks. They do not bleed when we finish. Your bite gives much pleasure."

She stepped towards him, recovering the lost distance. She wrapped her hands around his face and purred, "Prolonged bites will bring them fast." She shook her closed fist in the air as though jacking him off, smirking all the while. "Is too easy." She winked.

"But you must *remember,* never feed more than a minute. Absolutely *never* more than *two* minutes. They cannot handle excessive feedings. Is *very* dangerous. You must have care, until you learn control."

He nodded acceptance, but he didn't have a clue how he would be able to stop once he started. Her words invoked a wicked hunger. He wanted to snatch up her wrist and sink his teeth in again. He wanted to feed now, not in ten minutes, not for just one minute, and not in the hours they would waste cruising around town. He wanted it right this second! He wanted to drain someone dry of every last drop, and then tear into their flesh and squeeze it for more.

"Come, I will show you everything step by step. Watch, listen, and learn, *oui?*" She smiled, disarming his apprehensions and making it very difficult to think of anything beyond her angelic face just inches from his, holding his head in her hands.

As the idea sunk in that they were actually planning to go out on the town to *feed,* Aaron suddenly remembered his job at Bemichis. "Oh shit, I've gotta be at work tonight, I'm late. I'm scheduled to work all week. Bemichi is gonna kill me!" He felt panicky. He couldn't imagine how to reconcile all she had told him with his former life . He tried to step away from her, to make for the door. She halted him with her hands securely clamped on his head and a command snapped out in his face.

"Stop!"

That's exactly what he did. Stop. Right there in her hands, frozen solid. Panic struck with an explosion of adrenaline. He wanted to move, to run, to do something other than stand there, but his body wouldn't obey. She had him seized up dead in his tracks. His eyes could move, swirl around back and forth, side to side, up and down, but his body wouldn't do a damn thing. It was like being cast in concrete. He simply couldn't move, but he could talk.

"Please let me go. Please. I promise I won't do anything if you just let me go." He was heading over the edge of the abyss, staring into the bottomless well of madness. All reasoning processes washed away in the flush of panic.

"Silence!" she ordered him again, robbing him of the very last aspect of his free will, the power of speech. "You have been unconscious through the change. Is four nights past since the incident with the police. You have been dead to the world all this time." She gradually released the iron grip of her will over his body. The chains of her constrictive will lifted from all around his body. She let go of his face and took a step back. He knew she waited to see if he would lose it or accept the unpleasant reality of her domination.

He mumbled quietly, "Thank you."

He feared she might use her force of compulsion again. Life on eggshells. He had a heightened awareness of the slightest nuance of her displeasure that might cause a loss of his freedom of movement.

Watching him warily, she spoke in her weird, enigmatic way, "The world you once knew is no more for you." It was so true. The freedom he once knew was gone. He had begun to learn there were very finite limits to Michelle's patience. He took in the lesson and nodded his head silently.

Michelle put her arm through his and walked him to the door of the bedroom, keeping him close at hand. He stood there gawking as she pulled off her nightie and slipped into a dress right in front of him. She didn't need to command him to stay, or stop or whatever. She held his attention solidly with her perfectly sculpted body.

Heedless of her nudity, she gave him another tidbit of advice. "Don't concern yourself with anything else. Focus on the task at hand. Focus on what I say." He nodded like an idiot, barely hearing her words while she squirmed her picture perfect body into designer clothing worth more than his entire wardrobe.

Michelle had changed into a shiny silver, sleeveless dress, the loose fabric bunched at her hips, continuing a few more inches down as a skin-tight skirt barely covering the bottom curve of her ass. Braless, her nipples perked up, clearly visible through the almost sheer material. The effect was stunning. He would gladly do anything she asked.

In the elevator, her arm entwined around his, Michelle gave him that same sly smile, silently hinting at pleasures yet to come. Despite all the negative associations she represented in his life, he buzzed with anticipation and arousal.

As they left the apartment building, he noted the 90's décor, upscale for its time, now outdated. She had some money, but not too much. Definitely not Park Avenue. Despite the need for upgrades, her place was a huge step up from the telephone booth apartment he shared with Kyle. Much roomier and higher class than anything he could afford. He guessed Michelle's one bedroom suite cost her over two thousand a month.

In the taxi—making their way out into the New York nightlife— he spoke in hushed tones. "Michelle, I don't want to hurt people. Will they die from the feeding? Is it violent? Painful? What if I can't stop? What if I kill someone—by accident?" She cupped his face in her hands giving him a radiant smile. He completely forgot about all his myriad concerns. Her powerful physical presence, so close and intimate, wiped his mind of all else.

"That is so sweet. *Tu es très mignon.* Cute. Listen, and do not worry. I am not a murderer. We drink only a small sip. *Un apéritif, oui?* Is like shots of whiskey. Is not necessary to hurt anyone. Actually, they will enjoy this very much. You will see. I promise. *D'accord?*"

He nodded and breathed a sigh of relief, his tensions flowing out through her magical fingertips.

* * * *

CHAPTER 5

They stood outside a seedy strip club, the likes of which hadn't appeared in the A-lists for decades. As the taxi left, Aaron's anxiety returned. The neon sign out front snapped and crackled electric sex into the darkness of the surrounding night with a flashing declaration, "Girls, Girls, Girls." Felt like walking onto the film set of a bad 80's rock music video.

His low opinion of the place dropped several more notches upon entering. The smoky interior was covered in dark red upholstery and carpet, and populated with shifty-looking men stealing furtive glances in their direction. The kind of place you never wanted anyone you knew to catch you coming from or going to. He sensed relief from those who looked in his direction when they didn't recognize him. He sympathized with them. He felt the very same relief for not having recognized anyone.

There were several scantily-clad girls slinking around eyeing him and Michelle for prospective targets. The rest of the girls were sitting with men in various states of undress. The girl dancing on the raised platform in the center of the room undulated with the pole sliding up and down between her thighs in an imitation of sex. Her generous, naked breasts jiggled and bounced with each shift of direction.

Aaron was gradually buried in the crush of psychic waves of thoughts crashing over him from those in the room. The most prominent emotions were lust, desire, longing, and from the girls a lot of indifference and greed. A moan of confusion escaped his lips. Michelle gripped his arm tightly, maintaining a hold on him both physically and psychically. He felt the chains of her compulsive will power tightening around him.

She hissed in his ear, "Block it out!" With her compulsive prompt, a neat little bubble of silence slammed in place, effectively cutting off the bombardment of psychic noise. He realized she had forced him to cease scanning the surrounding people. He could have done it without her help. All he need do was quit reaching out. His own curiosity had triggered the barrage.

Once his internal storm quieted he noticed Michelle whispering to the doorman, who turned and led them to an alcove with several curtained areas. As they stood waiting, the doorman brought over a golden-skinned athletic girl. She had short, butch cut bleach-blond hair and wore only dental-floss thong bikini. Her booby tassels barely covering the tips of her nipples left nothing to the imagination. They followed her into one of the curtained booths and she closed the drapes behind them. Aaron reached out tentatively to the Butch's mind, trying to maintain a grip on his senses, trying to focus on her alone. It worked for the most part. He could hear her thoughts and the man in a nearby booth, but he wasn't swamped out by everyone in the building.

With his scanning somewhat under control, he delved straight into Butch's mind, rummaging around. She only had eyes for Michelle. Aaron might as well have been a shadow on the wall as far as Butch was concerned. She had a serious itch to get intimate with Michelle. She wasn't one of those bisexual girls who played with women at parties or stole kisses from their girlfriends. Butch was a full-on lesbian. She only stripped for men the money. She had no attraction for men at all. It was relatively easy for Butch to tactfully avoid men's advances, pushing their hands away—occasionally swatting them away. The whole transaction was strictly business.

Butch finally turned her fake, I-think-you're-so-sexy smile towards him, but her thoughts centered on Michelle.

"Are you looking for a two on one?" Butch asked with a raised eyebrow. She hoped not. She wanted Michelle all to herself. It was a rare treat when a woman as beautiful as Michelle visited a dive like this.

Michelle reassured her, "*Non*, just me." Butch smiled genuinely as she moved towards Michelle. She planned to have some real fun on this one, maybe even break the cardinal rule, *no sex*.

The girls sat down together on the semicircular seating. Butch locked eyes with Michelle, never looking away. She began to dance for her, moving to the rhythm of the music that pervaded the entire club. Within a moment she had climbed up onto Michelle's lap, swaying and grinding her hips, her legs spread-eagle. She stroked her fingertips over Michelle's nipples, smiling as they perked and hardened with her touch—*it was okay to touch them, but they can't touch back*. He sat down on the seat a couple feet away from the show, his eyes glued to the girls. This was definitely the most erotic thing he'd ever witnessed. He was already rock hard in his pants, and the action hadn't begun yet.

Michelle maintained eye contact with Butch the entire time, inviting her in with an unmistakable come-hither look. It was one of those *Come into my parlor, said the spider to the fly* kinda moments. Michelle seduced the seducer. The girl didn't have a clue she was sitting in the lap of a predator.

Michelle leaned forward whispering to the girl with a hypnotic suggestion, "Come closer." Butch leaned in, and Michelle struck swift and hard, biting her neck with a soft, wet, sucking sound. As Michelle clutched the girl to her, her arm locked around the back of her neck, Butch began grinding hard and fast against Michelle's lap. Butch breathed in desperate gasps and hit two quick, heaving spasms. Grinding and humping atop Michelle's lap, she cried out, "Oh my God! Oh, oh God. Yes!"

Michelle released her bite as the girl slumped against her chest, panting heavily. It took Butch a moment to regain her composure, and then she stood up on shaky legs and stepped away from Michelle's lap with a shy, embarrassed grin. Michelle stood up face to face with her, maintaining that freaky, unblinking gaze, and handed her a couple twenties. "That will be all for now. Send another girl for him."

Michelle gestured towards Aaron, who Butch had literally forgotten was there. Butch was sorely disappointed to be summarily dismissed so quickly. She wasn't used to being treated that way by the usual club crowd. She found it humbling to be on the receiving end of this kind of treatment.

As soon as Butch left the curtained booth Michelle explained, "Is all eye contact. Do not break eye contact. Hold her with your eyes and tell her what you want. She will be all yours. Do exactly as I did. Release the bite after one minute. The girls come very close here. Is very easy."

Next entered a cute, brown-haired, brown-eyed girl, with a sweet, shy smile. She looked really young, younger than Aaron. Michelle gestured in his direction and the girl asked, "What do you have in mind?"

"A lap dance." He tried not to smile like an idiot at the girl.

She took off her robe setting it to the side. "My name is Lisa."

She wore nothing but one of those dental-floss bikinis, same as the previous girl. Her body was soft and curvy without the athletic, hard edge of the Butch that danced for Michelle. In truth she looked barely of age.

Lisa moved slowly and sensually to the music, sliding up into his lap. He held her gaze as she mounted him. His erection punched up the crotch of his pants, *pitching a tent.* Lisa began rubbing her breasts up his chest while curving her warm, wet center, back and forth over his raised pants, giving a constant massage to the tip of his engorged cock. He read her sincere desire to screw him silly right there, rules be damned. She was completely enthralled, and all he'd done was stare at her.

As she dry-humped him with a wonderfully agonizing pelvic grind, she had slid into biting distance. His senses heightened with arousal. Lisa's pulse beat throughout her body with a fluttering at her throat just under the skin. He felt an itch coming from his fangs. They were fully exposed and *needed* to be sunk into this girl. He *so* wanted to take a chunk out of her.

27

Michelle gave a slight nod he perceived as *the signal*, and he lashed out to bite down on that beautiful, little pounding pulse point. It seemed the most natural thing in the world–like he'd been doing this all his life. The instinct and know-how to bite was deeply ingrained into his new psyche. It was official. He could no longer deny the truth. Aaron was now a vampire.

His fangs punctured her skin with a yucky squish sound. Lisa tensed up at the initial sting of the bite, and then relaxed as his venom dumped a wonderful magic flow of endorphins into her bloodstream. Her blood coated his tongue in delicious syrup. He sucked hard and fast, gulping whole mouthfuls. Her strong little heart pumped blood just as fast as he could swallow. The experience was exquisite. Simply the richest, sweetest delight of flavor he had ever known.

With the blood flow came a new flood of Lisa's emotions, passions, and a sense of her very life essence. His psychic connection sunk in deep with the flow of her blood. He immersed in her psyche, everything Lisa. She washed away his sense of identity. There was only Lisa and her fantastic euphoria brought on by the venom coursing through her blood stream. Lisa panted and gasped. Her whole body rocked with the force of her grinding thrusts on his lap, her entry engulfing the tip of his cock.

He felt psychic waves of ecstasy pouring off her in her venom-soaked climax. As her wetness gushed onto his pants, soaking his erection, he penetrated another inch, having sex fully-clothed.

Lisa's peak struck again and again, each eruption slamming gasps and cries from her lips. The combination of the blood high, Lisa's psychic ecstasy pouring over him, and his near climax, hit a total sensory overload. This was a divine religious experience. The kingdom of Heaven shone down with all its hosts and choir singing praises to God.

Michelle shut the pearly gates to Heaven in Aaron's face with her command, "No more, stop now!"

He released Lisa involuntarily. She collapsed against his chest with heaving gasps and pathetic whimpering sounds at each exhale. Her body molded to his torso like gelatin. She shook and quivered from the intense life-changing experience she'd undergone.

Lisa looked upon Aaron in adoration, kissing his neck and face, caressing him lovingly. After she stopped shaking and moaning with orgasmic aftershocks, Michelle lifted Lisa off Aaron from behind like a mother removing a babe from her father's arms. Lisa looked as though she would leap back into his lap, like she couldn't stand to be apart from him. Michelle held Lisa's gaze, mesmerizing her while shoving twenty dollar bills into her hand.

She commanded Lisa, "Go to the restroom and clean up." Lisa suddenly remembered herself and realized her behavior with embarrassment. She rushed out the curtain towards the back rooms.

Michelle leaped toward Aaron hissing. "*Imbécile*, look what you have done!"

His eyes hurled daggers of malice. He considered jumping up to throttle her on the spot. He had never experienced such severe aching sexual frustration in all his life. He understood now what it meant when people joked about *blue balls*. Michelle had ordered him to stop mere seconds before he popped off. He was rock-hard, aching, and frustrated as hell. No happy endings for Aaron Pilan.

Michelle threw a napkin at him from her purse and spit rapid fire. "Wipe yourself. Hurry! We must go now!" He looked at her as if she was insane. How could she force him to leave here after what just happened?

"*Tu es bêtes comme te pieds!*" She glared right back at him, letting him know he was no more intelligent than the bottom of his feet. "I will explain once we leave. Hurry, she will return any minute. She is now your *bloodslave*. We cannot stay!"

Exactly as Michelle predicted, Lisa caught up with them at the exit just before they could escape. Lisa latched onto him with a mile wide smile, slipping her hand into his pocket with her phone number, stroking him intimately from inside his pants.

Lisa looked him in the eyes with her free hand holding his chin and said, "Call me ... seriously. I want you to call me tonight. I don't say this to men who come in here. I'm saying it now. I'm totally serious. I mean it. You better not forget me, okay?" She seemed to consider for a second then continued.

"It's not about money. I don't want your money. I want to see you again tonight. I'm off work in four and a half hours, at three a.m. You can meet me in the parking lot." She begged him with her eyes and stroked the length of him to prove the sincerity of her invitation. "I don't even know your name." She gave him a puppy dog *needy* look.

"My name is Aaron. And I'll call you. Don't worry, okay?"

He grinned like an idiot. She had stroked him the entire time. She had his cock so hard he considered throwing her down on the floor right there to have his way with her. He suspected she'd probably let him—he held that much influence over her. Having this kind of power over a beautiful, young, half-naked stripper was a heady experience. It felt fantastic to finally be the one in control of the situation.

She aligned her body with his, pressing up on him with all her lovely curvaceous parts. "Please don't forget me, okay?" She looked ready to cry.

He almost begged Michelle to let him stay, but thought better of it. She seemed pretty pissed off, and he suspected he'd catch an earful on the way out. He reassured Lisa twice more that he *would not forget her* while Michelle dragged him out the door to their next set of adventures in vampiring.

In the taxi, Michelle turned to him with a steady, controlling hand on his thigh. "I know how you feel, but listen. What you did to that girl was horrible. Your bite is like heroin. You have very strong venom." She held his gaze as she flicked her fingertip at his fangs, pointing out the obvious.

"Is very intense sexual excitement. Too much is instant addiction, just like heroin. You must never feed more than two minutes or you risk the addiction. You held this poor girl for too long. She had many orgasms, *oui?*" He nodded, admitting the truth of her words.

"She will be anemic for days. You took too much. But the real *problème* is her addiction for *you.*" She poked her finger at his chest in accusation. "It is psychological and physical addiction. You must *never* bite this girl again. You must *never* see this girl again. We cannot return tonight. If given the chance, she will pursue and stalk you. You have marked this girl forever. She will think of you always. Is very important you understand. Is a serious *problème. Très mal.*"

Michelle paused to let the import of her words sink in. "She is now your *bloodslave.* She will suffer withdrawals from you for weeks. Her pain will be constant. Depression may drive her to suicide. You should be ashamed."

He was, at this point, quite ashamed, yet still very frustrated from the whole experience. "Why didn't you tell me before? Why did you let me do this?" He felt like a complete asshole once he understood the full ramifications of what he'd done to Lisa, and he wasn't above laying the blame on Michelle's shoulders for her part.

Michelle cupped his face with her hands. "*Oui,* is my fault. You were not truly prepared, but now you know. There will be no *excuse* next time. You must *never* make this mistake again. Let this be a *lesson.*" She was dead serious. He caught the flow of her emotions leaking through their psychic bond. She had an unwavering resolve to ensure that Aaron *never* abused another woman—a deadly resolve.

He followed this thread of thought in Michelle's mind via their connection. This bloodslave thing was a real sore spot for her. She'd seen it happen before. He caught a shadowy glimpse of numerous faces. Thin, emaciated faces. A great heap of sadness and grief hid just under the surface of her mind. He almost reached into that pile of writhing snakes, but thought better of it. He shied away from her pain and leaned back to the other side of the bench seat.

She held him with her calm, unnerving gaze. He'd dug a little too deep, traveling through unwelcome corridors of her mind.

"I will do *whatever* is necessary to be certain you respect them. Do not test me." There it was in her mind, plain as day for Aaron to read. She would ensure he was careful with the women they fed from, even if it meant killing him. This mistake was on her, a freebie. If he continued abusing women it would get serious. A non-negotiable issue. He sensed a dark gruesome history underlay Michelle's strong feelings. She had been a victim.

* * * *

CHAPTER 6

Aaron stood beside Michelle on the roof of her apartment building, looking out over the city lights, breathing in the smells, listening to the night sounds of passing cars and people living normal lives. To his enhanced vision the night sky-line and rooftops glowed with illumination. He could see everything, almost as if it were daylight. His night vision was superb.

Standing there looking down on the world, he felt divorced from the human race, an outsider peeking in windows but never truly entering within. He'd felt this way before, especially after his father's death, but now it was real. He was truly disconnected from all of humanity.

The tangs of city life in all their ripe flavor drifted on the air; remnants of meals cooked, unwashed sweaty bodies, sewer vents and auto exhaust. He took it all in, identifying each scent with the understanding that he would never again be mired in such things, human things. It was exciting, but equally intimidating. He had no one in the world but this strange woman he called *Master*. His father had been gone for years, and his mother bailed on him shortly thereafter. Relations with Kyle and Delia and all those other *people* who were once a significant part of his life couldn't continue. He was detached from the world and all its problems, and it felt kinda ... *good*. He felt free, like a great weight had lifted from his shoulders, all expectations gone. There was no one to answer to, no one to buy beer for, no one except Michelle. She reminded him of this new weight of expectation as she squeezed his hand demanding attention.

She'd brought them to the roof but hadn't bothered to explain why. She turned to him, "Is a good time to learn how your new body moves. Is purely instinctual. Don't think too much. Watch me, I go first, then is your turn."

With that, she did the craziest thing he'd ever seen. She stepped right off the roof of her twenty story apartment building and landed gracefully on the fire escape catwalk two stories below. No ceremony, no warning. She did it like it was the thing to do when standing at the edge of a building. Like the chicken that crossed the road *to get to the other side*. She touched down as if nothing. Virtually no impact from her landing.

Michelle continued doing the impossible by leaping across the alleyway, flying fifty feet through the air, and gradually descending in a graceful arc until she landed on the wall of the neighboring concrete building. As she hit, she crouched down into the impact and vaulted off the wall back out into the alley for another graceful arc of descent. She glided down at an angle into a textbook perfect landing precisely at the fire escape catwalk outside her apartment window. With each of these artfully executed maneuvers she descended lower and lower as though traveling down a switch-back trail from a mountain top.

After all that, she had the audacity to lean out over the catwalk railing and look up at him with an innocent smile. "Now is your turn."

He was stunned into silence. He stood there with a dumb expression, his mouth open in awe. She was a friggin' Jedi master, a super hero (heroine). Spider Woman, Cat Woman, and the Black Widow all rolled into one. And just how the hell was he supposed to keep up? How could she expect him to do that shit?

When he regained the ability to speak he protested loudly, "No. Fucking. Way!"

She had that I'm-not-playing-with-you-*Imbécile* look.

He tried to reason with her, "Maybe this is another one of those situations I'm not quite ready for yet. I honestly don't see how I can do that."

"You can do this, no *problème*. Your body knows how to move. Is like breathing. Don't think about it!" She smiled again. Wonder Woman hadn't even broken a sweat. She stood there with an expectant look.

"No way José. No can do." He shook his head. A dread sensation settled in the pit of his gut. *She's fucking serious.* She really wanted him to jump. Her impatience with him broadcast over their psychic bond. He sensed what she was about to do a split second before she did it. That was all the warning he got.

"Jump now and follow in my steps!" Michelle spoke in that strange resonant timbre of command and he jumped off the side of a twenty story building involuntarily.

"Oh shit oh shit oh *shiiiit!*"

Much to his surprise, he made a decent landing on the catwalk below, same as Michelle. The thirty foot drop felt like only three feet. Continuing on with the *follow in my steps* command, he leapt across to the neighboring building, descending in an arc. He basically followed Michelle's path, but had underestimated his strength. When he hit the wall of the neighboring building feet first, the cement cracked a ten foot wide spider-web. He launched off the wall exactly as she had done, mimicking her movements and following her path of descent, but a large piece of the wall dislodged behind him and fell to the alley below. He was far more powerful than he knew.

In his final maneuver, he miscalculated again, using way too much force for his jump. Instead of landing on the catwalk as she had, he plowed straight into her. Of course, she saw him coming and intercepted him. She spun and slammed him into the wall, redirecting his force and knocking the wind out of him with a bone-crushing thud. He thought he heard something crack, but he wasn't sure if it was his back or the wall. Felt like his back, maybe his ribs. It took a moment to catch his breath past the sharp pains in his back and chest.

"See, I told you! Next time listen when I tell you something!" she snapped with a smug grin. "Stupid Americans. Think they know everything!" she spit in derision.

"*Tu me pèles le jonc!*" She let him know his behavior had gotten on her nerves in her not-so-cute-anymore French accent. With this she heaved Aaron over her shoulder, spinning 180 degrees. He went flying out into the alleyway tumbling end-over-end, headed straight for the pavement. He had absolutely no forewarning. She'd cleverly concealed her intention to toss him over the railing of the catwalk like yesterday's newspaper.

"Oh Fuck! Oh my god!"

Though he had no warning, he recovered quickly. As she had attempted to explain earlier, he instinctively knew how to manage the fall. Like a cat with nine lives and inhuman agility, he twisted and turned in the air to bring his spinning momentum aligned for a feet first landing. He dropped into a tight little crouch with the impact, his hands touching down for balance. He fell four stories without injury.

Michelle shocked him further by issuing another compulsory command, "Come to me now!"

He leaped into the air, snatched up the bottom rung of the ladder twelve feet off the ground, and scaled the fire escape. He pounded up the stairways at a breakneck velocity any fireman would be proud to witness. He reached Michelle on the fourth story in mere seconds. The little psychotic witch welcomed him with a smile.

He watched her with trepidation. She damn near killed him twice in the span of a couple minutes. He couldn't decide whether he should laugh, scream, cry, or beg.

As she opened the window to let him into her bedroom, she mocked him. "*Est-ce que tu as le démon de midi?*" Having a mid-life crisis?

He followed her inside and wisely kept his mouth shut. She went about the apartment doing this, that, and the other thing, girly things. She kept her distance, letting him calm down. How courteous and considerate of her.

Sitting on Michelle's bed, steeped in the scents of her perfume and other distinctive body odors, he attempted to reconcile his new reality. He was now a blood-sucking vampire with amazing physical strength and agility, and some rather interesting talents for seduction. He had exceptionally acute senses and could read the minds of those nearby. He was a slave to the will of his drop-dead gorgeous—though slightly psychotic—vampire master whom he found difficult to trust and was fast learning to fear. The question was how did he feel about it?

Stuck. Stuck on her, and stuck with her.

She seduced him effortlessly every time she spoke in that alluring-irritating-cute-sexy-maddening French accent. Despite all the reasons he shouldn't let emotion color his dealings with Michelle, it was too late. That war had been lost before it began.

Love at first site.

Whether she was a guardian angel or a demoness didn't matter. He was smitten, infatuated, and he could hardly keep his eyes off her. She had him good, right where she wanted him, and there wasn't a damn thing he could do about it. She owned him; body, heart, and soul, and she hadn't even fucked him yet. He knew she didn't feel the same way about him. He was a *trainee*, a liability, not a man to love or respect.

All things considered, he decided it wise to conceal his thoughts deep in his mental vault and try not to wear his foolish heart on his sleeve. He might be her slave, but that didn't mean he was without pride.

She slipped up on him quietly, and her fingers traced a pattern over his shoulder, sending a zing straight to his groin. "Are you planning to scowl for the rest of the night or are we going to have sex?" She gave him her *Helen of Troy* smile that could launch a thousand ships, sending them all to their demise.

While doing a double take, he snapped, "You just shoved me off the roof of a building. Can I have a chance to get my head straight?" As her words penetrated his frustration, he began to warm to all the wonderful possibilities that stemmed from her blatant proposition.

After a minute of silence he back tracked, "Look, I'll admit the roof thing was exciting and kind of fun and … I don't even have a scratch on me so … I guess there's no harm, no foul."

"Does this mean we are going to have sex now?" She slipped her fingers through his hair seductively, massaging his scalp in wonderful little circles. "I promise I will not order you around … this time … *Ça va?*" She gave him her most innocent look while wrapping her arms around him to bring his head down to her breasts.

"Well, since you put it that way." he mumbled into her mostly uncovered cleavage. He couldn't say no, didn't even want to say no. Why bother pretending? For once he was getting laid and he didn't even have to beg for it.

They could let bygones be bygones for the moment. She wasn't gonna force him, or so she said. But then maybe that sort of force wouldn't be so horrible. As the saying goes, *you can't rape the willing*. Michelle took control of the situation when she lashed out to bite him on the neck. He reacted without thinking. It was an instinctual thing that just happened. He wrapped around her and bit her right back.

He realized she'd been counting on it. She wasn't the least bit surprised. He fell into a heavenly bliss of feeding and drug-like euphoria as the venom-induced ecstasy brought him to climax simultaneously with Michelle. She purred her pleasure at him, grinding her moist hot crotch all over his leg.

"*Oh oui, encore!* It has been such a long time since I felt this way. Only with vampires can it be so ... mmm ... there is nothing quite like it ... is the *sense de la vie!*" She licked his blood from her lips and caressing his hard cock from the outer bulge of his pants.

His mind whirled with the overwhelming power of her presence and touch. He felt like a kid in a candy store. He could scarce believe his good fortune at being the object of this super model's seductive attentions.

"You know I'm not really experienced." It slipped from his mouth without any thought, his venom-saturated loins speaking before his brain kicked in. As the words tumbled out, he mentally ordered himself to shut-up.

"*Oui.* Is no *problème.* I will teach you everything in time. You must trust me. I know you don't, but you have no choice." She stated this matter-of-factly while unbuttoning his pants with quick, deft movements. The girl was an old pro.

As she undressed him, she explained, "I know how the world sees French women. They say we are sexually liberated. *Oui?*" He nodded slowly, uncertain where she was headed with this revelation.

"The truth, we are actually quite traditional. We like the old-fashioned courtesies. *Comprends?*" He nodded again, entranced as her hands undid buttons and zippers and slid his shirt off his chest.

"I expect the simple courtesies like opening doors, pulling out chairs, changing light bulbs, unplugging the nasty sink drains, answering phones to fend off telemarketers ... sending flowers for no particular reason. And most important, you must give the courtesy of allowing me to orgasm *first.*"

"That's the French way?" He swallowed with an audible gulp as he stepped out of his pants and underwear. He had never been naked with a woman with the lights on, it was kinda nerve-wracking.

"*Oui.* Classical European etiquette. This one time I will make an exception, for the purpose of our lesson."

She gently pushed him back onto the bed and proceeded to work him by hand. She knew exactly what he wanted, how he wanted it, where he wanted it. She plucked it straight from his mind. Within moments she worked him to a back-arching explosive peak, robbing him of the ability to think or speak. This was achieved in the same impersonal manner she had adopted as his official teacher of the fine arts of vampirism.

She gave him a short minute to compose himself while cleaning her hands methodically. Then she stepped out of her dress and stood before him in nothing but the tiniest pair of black thong panties he'd ever seen. He grew rock hard all over again staring at her fabulous body. She had to be completely shaved. No way hair could hide under her minuscule fishing-line panties.

She represented every ridiculous Hollywood-inspired fantasy he could recall. He'd jerked off to far less attractive swimsuit models as a teenager.

"Oh my god, you are so beautiful." He blurted it out like a lovesick idiot.

She worked the black string down her hips and stepped up to greet him and his swollen erection thumping against his belly.

"Now is my turn."

She took his hand and directed his fingers down along her smooth belly to the soft mound between her legs. Her delicate folds were warm, slick, swollen, flowing over his fingertips like liquid silk. She showed him the key points of female anatomy that must be attended to and duly appreciated.

Following her lead, he learned all the sensitive erogenous zones of Michelle's body, each touch eliciting a corresponding musical sound. She opened her psychic link, allowing him to feel all that she felt, to reinforce her instructions with her response to his hands, tongue and teeth.

"*Oui*, there … and here. *Oui, oui!* Faster, harder, don't stop!"

He found the noises of her pleasure fascinating. She was not a quiet lover. Michelle made wonderful French music with her moans, groans, and sighs—and the occasional growl or grunt.

"Oohh … Ahhh … OH! Aiieeee … Oooff … aarrggghh … Shoosh!" Her hands gripped his wrist, humping his fingers without reservation. Her crescendo finished in a screaming orgasm of, "*Oooouuiii!*"

After catching her breath, she crawled over the top of him. Unsure what she had planned next, he asked, "Do you want to be on top?"

Fangs fully extended, she grinned gleaming white and licked her lips. "*Bien sûr.*"

Legs wide open, she impaled herself all the way down in one smooth move. Michelle was indeed an old pro. She rode him with the enthusiasm of veteran porn-stars, gliding up and down, popping and grinding her hips to get every last inch of him. Soon her pace and force reached that of hard, pounding, pelvis-crushing slams. It hurt, with her preternatural strength and vigor, but the intensity of their dual climaxes wiped away all discomfort.

Breathing heavily with a glazed smile on her face, Michelle hauled him over to the side, rolling with him. He ending up on top with her legs locked around him in a professional wrestler's hold. She bit him for a moment allowing the magic of her venom to engorge his arousal. He grew a full size erection inside of her within seconds. Without speaking a word she instructed him in a series of motions through their psychic bond. She taught him all the different angles and methods of intimacy from this position. She showed him exactly where she wanted it, how fast, how hard, and rewarded him with little squeals and grunts as he hit her spot. Her educational series took them through another mutual mind-numbing orgasm punctuated by episodes of mutual biting. They screwed until he could take no more.

"Please … let's give it a rest … it hurts," he admitted sheepishly as he tried to catch his breath after the umpteenth round of sex. She surveyed his cock as it started going limp.

She rewarded him with another of her glorious smiles. "*D'accord*, that will do for now. We have all the time in the world for more lessons."

* * * *

In the morning just before sunrise, as they lay tangled together in bed after three hours of blood-sucking-mind-blowing sex, Michelle considered her situation. She knew he was infatuated with her. He couldn't hide it. But he was very young, and such things are common with inexperienced men. Michelle thought it possible she might eventually develop some sentiment for him. He had a certain boyish charm, he seemed so guileless. He was not a deceptive or malicious person. Those two points alone were enough to hold her attention. Such men were a rare find in this culture of artificial personalities. He was genuine, maybe a bit too naive, but still genuine.

She had found him fresh and clean, uncontaminated by the decadence of the New York scene. Michelle assumed it was only a matter of time before these qualities she admired would dissipate. Life had a way of stripping away luxuries like innocence and naiveté. She would lose this fresh young boy eventually. She intended to fully enjoy him while it lasted. Quite a nice change from the men she normally met in her line of work.

Emotional attachment was the issue now. She couldn't really afford to get too close to him. If he started to turn sour and violent, like her former master, she'd be forced to deal with it. She couldn't allow her feelings to sway her judgment. She had to stay objective about killing him. For the meantime, she was willing to discount her lingering attraction to him as nothing more than the sated after-effects of great sex.

She wasn't really willing to examine her feelings in any great depth. It seemed wiser to maintain his fear and respect, keeping strong emotions out of the equation. Sex, for her, was not complicated, especially with Aaron, who unlike the weak humans, could actually keep up with her physically in the bedroom.

However, emotional commitments were very complicated. She hoped to maintain a balance in the master/slave relationship without becoming too overbearing and avoiding emotional involvement with her slave. It would be a challenge, but she was up to the task. Michelle prided herself on her rigid self-control.

* * * *

THE NIGHTLIFE NEW YORK

CHAPTER 7

Police Chief Schueller yelled in Detective Konowicz's face, "I know this chic didn't go ballistic on you two for no good reason. I know what the fuck you were doin'! Don't lie to me!"

Konowicz spluttered, "She was on drugs, crack or meth or somethin'. I'm totally serious, Chief. She was all speeded out, a real public safety hazard!"

"You're gonna find this girl, and I will find out the truth! If I hear you were hittin' her up for money you're gone. I told you last time, if another hooker files a report against you, it's over. Not even the union will be able to save your ass."

"Yes, sir. No problem. I'll get right on it." Konowicz shuffled out of the office.

"I know you will, and you're gonna bring her back here safe and sound, in one piece, so I can talk to her! Not a mark on her, you hear!" Konowicz didn't acknowledge. He kept on rolling out the door.

Schueller shook his head, a temple-pounding headache coming on. He recalled a book he read back in the 80's called *The Peter Principle*, about employees having a tendency to rise to the highest level of incompetence. The book described how people hit the ceiling of their careers due to the inability to competently manage their responsibilities. Schueller had become convinced that Dr. Lawrence J. Peter was a prophet. The good doc must have foreseen the life and times of Scott Konowicz when he wrote his book.

This was the defining characteristic of Konowicz's life, incompetence. He considered Konowicz a shining example of the golden age of mediocrity celebrated across America today. His exquisite failures reached into every facet of his life, leaving no stone unturned, no accomplishment untainted. His spectacular divorce and lack of children was a shining trophy on the mantle of failure he donned upon his shoulders each day on his way out the door to work (after spiking his coffee with the cheapest bottle of rum available at the corner liquor store).

Konowicz ate, slept, and drank of ineptitude to such excess that it rivaled his alcohol consumption. When Schueller confronted Konowicz four years ago about his alcoholism, trying to offer the idiot some help, Konowicz replied, "No Alcoholics Anonymous for me, no sir. That shit's for quitters! The only twelve steps I need are the steps leading from the car to the checkout counter of the liquor store!" The idiot had laughed it off. *You can lead a horse to water but you can't make it drink.*

Schueller watched through the blinds of his office window as Konowicz approached his fat sidekick, Oberman. They couldn't be more different looking, and yet they were two sides of the same coin. They matched each other nearly point for point. Their lives were like mirror images of one another. They damn near finished each other's sentences.

Both detectives shared the same tendency for corruption and bribery. This was the primary reason Schueller had pared them up as partners six years ago. Better to let two bad apples rot together rather than watch them pervert others on the force with their corrupt influence.

Schueller sighed, rubbed a hand across his face and mumbled to himself, "They're poster children for labor union reform. If the union can make allowance for their continued employment, it must be fundamentally flawed."

Schueller was well aware that both detectives spent their unproductive days skating on the minimum effort required to keep their jobs. They played the Rodney Dangerfield role, *I get no respect!* He also knew they spent their lonely nights shaking down pimps, prostitutes, and drug dealers for a little bonus pay, a few hundred here, a few hundred there. Both having hit the limits of their careers years ago, they took it upon themselves to get ahead the old-fashioned way: threats, blackmail, extortion, and coercion.

Schueller sincerely hoped he could finagle a signed statement from this mystery blonde and put an end to both their careers. It took a lot of dirt to get rid of an NYPD officer, but those two had been pushing the limits of tolerable police behavior for far too long. The office of internal affairs had a dossier on both of them longer than most criminal rap sheets.

* * * *

Detective Konowicz was not a happy man. Every time he spoke, turned his head, tried to eat or drink, his nose spiked pain throughout his skull, causing a series of throbbing waves of misery. His Oxycontin pain pills kicked in with a nice buzz, but the catcalls and teasing from his fellow officers left him with a foul attitude.

"Hey, Konowicz, is it true you had your ass handed to you by a hundred pound bimbo?"

"Hey! We should put the bimbo on *The Jerry Springer Show* with Konowicz and Oberman. After she's done kicking their asses all over the stage, she can do a number on the stripper pole!" This knee-slapper had them all busting a gut, tears streaming down their faces.

"I heard she zapped Oberman right in da freakin' nuts wit' your piece. You gotta give her points for originality on that one!"

"I bet the chief had their balls for breakfast over that shit!" The legend of their confrontation with the blonde grew with each retelling.

"Everybody's a fuckin' stand-up comedian," Konowicz grumbled under his breath so as to avoid inciting further comment. The incident with the little blonde cunt was the most recent humiliation he'd endured, but it was a symptom of a much larger problem. This event sat atop a heaping list of embarrassing disappointments. The list stretched back over the decades, extending throughout twenty-two years of an unrewarding and meritless police career.

Life had not been good to Konowicz, but his police work provided a nice outlet for the anger and frustration. Out on the streets, he and Oberman didn't take any crap from criminals unfortunate enough to land in their path. Especially the prostitutes. Bust a few heads, shake down some whores, collect a few dollars, grab onto some new names and do it all over again. Whether by cash or services rendered, the girls always paid. Konowicz had the unbreakable power of the law behind him. Nobody dared to defy him. Nobody but this bimbo.

Saddled with a broken nose for all his co-workers to see and appreciate had enraged him to the point of murder. Konowicz planned to get that little bitch one way or another. It wasn't just business, it had become a personal vendetta. She'd never see the chief. There would be no signed statements. He wasn't a fool, and he surely wasn't going down for some hot piece of tail with a bullshit complaint of extortion.

Konowicz fantasized long and hard about horribly unspeakable things he might do to her before he killed her. Oh, how she would beg and plead. She'd do anything he wanted. *Anything.* She'd probably try to pay him off first. That's how it usually went when things got rough. He might even let her scrape up some money before he finished the job … drag it out a little longer. Konowicz got down with some serious planning. He put more effort into his plans for revenge than his own career.

He needed to be certain Oberman would go along with it. Konowicz approached Oberman privately during lunch at the greasy spoon diner they frequented.

"Hey … we gonna fuck dis chick up when we find her? We ain't takin' no prisoners right?" Konowicz spoke in hushed tones, his plugged sinuses added a nasal whine to his voice.

"Yeah, no problem. This bitch is gonna wake up dead in a dumpster by the time we're finished," Oberman confirmed with a malicious gleam in his eye.

Konowicz had expected as much. They were both on the same track. Business as usual. "You get the artist's rendering yet?" Konowicz whined.

"Yeah, it looks close enough. Where do you wanna start?"

"I was thinkin' we could hit up Talco. See if he knows anything about her."

"I bet he knows somethin'. We'll catch him tonight. He owes us one after the last stunt he pulled."

"Gotta figure a package that sweet turns a few heads. We're gonna find her real soon. She must be workin' with somebody. Chick like that ain't walkin' the streets alone."

Konowicz nodded. With the network of pimps and prostitutes they had access to it was only a matter of time before they found her.

* * * *

Talco stood at the entrance to Chandler's Bar and Grill waiting for the arrival of Oberman and Konowicz, a.k.a. *Los Demonios*. Everything involving those two A-holes equated to a deal with the devil. He wondered how he'd ever rid himself of their tyrannical influence on his life. He couldn't imagine anything short of killing them that would free him, and he wasn't a murderer. A pimp, a bastard, a felon on probation, he fit all these descriptions, but not a killer. Not yet.

"It's about fuckin' time you showed up. Been waitin' for twenty-five minutes, mane! You think I got nothing better to do?" Talco complained in his heavy Puerto Rican accent.

"Relax, sit down, have a beer. Ain't you ever heard, patience is a fuckin' virtue?" Konowicz gestured to a corner booth in the bar. He continued, "You're too high strung. Look at Oberman here, that's what happens with too much stress."

"Yeah fuck you too. Your ugly mug ain't winning any beauty contests," Oberman retorted at Konowicz.

Talco looked at Oberman's scratched face and Konowicz's broken nose. He prayed to the Blessed Virgin he would never allow himself to deteriorate so badly that he resembled either of them. His sleek, fit, twenty-seven year old, golden-tanned Puerto Rican body was in its prime, and he intended to keep it that way for years to come. To Talco, Oberman's overweight fifty-plus years of bulk with heavy bulldog jowls and beady eyes was the worst condition a man could be in. Konowicz, although trim, was plenty undesirable in his own gaunt, balding way.

They looked like a wicked version of *Laurel and Hardy* with Brooklyn accents, heavy drinking problems, and noses for smelling out nasty business. Somehow, their indecent ventures always seemed to find a way from their hands into his lap.

Los Demonios ordered rounds of beers and burgers. *I'll be paying the tab. Those putos didn't ask for separate checks.*

"I got somethin' here for ya. Look at this." Oberman handed the artist's rendering of a blond woman to Talco. "You recognize her?" Talco looked over the drawing for a moment and shook his head.

"She's workin' the streets. She's been seen in the last week by Palmetto and 60th. Claims to be workin' alone, but she's a hot little bitch, and it don't make no sense that she'd be out there on her own."

Talco sensed something personal involved in this. He got a really bad feeling. There was more to this girl than they were telling him. He speculated she had something to do with the scratches across Oberman's face and silently praised any woman brave enough to fight back. The sad part, this chick was already fucked. She just didn't know it yet. You do not go head-to-head with NYPD, a serious mistake.

Konowicz stared hard at Talco, making certain to impart the severity of his request. "This baby here's got your name all over it. You find her and we're square for the last payment you owe. Think you can handle it?"

Perhaps the girl was involved in something serious, heroin or something. Maybe she needed to be taken in. Maybe it was legit. "I'll ask around, see what I can find out. I'll put in the time. I'll try, but I can't guarantee anything. And what if I can't find her? All this for nothing? You still gonna be on my case, man? I gotta life too, a wife and kid!"

"Hey, you better remember a few things. You gotta do everything you can to protect that sweet little chica at home. You get popped on a probation violation and you'll be doing twenty-four months. That ain't gonna be so good for the mamasita. Maybe she's gonna have to work the streets again to pay the bills. You wanna see that? You wanna see her on her back again while you're locked up?" Konowicz threatened in his nasal voice.

He knew these weren't idle threats. With nothing but a phone call to his probation officer from either detective, Talco would be immediately thrown in lockup. Since he was already convicted, and on probation, he had no rights to speak of. And he wasn't exactly *keeping his nose clean*, running a prostitution racket on the side. His life had been a living hell from the moment the detectives had pressured one of his girls into revealing the name of her employer. They had owned his ass ever since.

Talco seriously considered the idea of killing these two disgusting pigs. They could sit here in front of him, calmly drinking beer at his expense, and discuss the ruination of his life. His temper flared, his fists and jaw clenched tight. Generations of hot-blooded Puerto Rican genetics warred against his better judgment. Evita warned him constantly to calm down and think before acting. He had to cool down, that's what Evita always said, "Cool it pappy, te quiero mucho. No te asustes."

It was his hot blood that put him in prison the first time, after he beat some asshole senseless for smacking around Evita when she refused him anal sex. She'd been so appreciative that she'd stood by Talco's side through every court appointment while he was prosecuted for aggravated assault. In the face-off of an obnoxious fast-talking Puerto Rican vs. a respectable white businessman, the jury's verdict against Talco was a foregone conclusion.

The one witness whose testimony could've brought to light all the mitigating factors in his defense had remained silent. Talco refused to let Evita take the stand. She'd wanted to defend him, to return the favor, she'd begged Talco to let her testify. But the prosecutor knew the score. He'd threatened to have Evita deported back to Colombia if she testified. Talco had forced her to stay out of it to protect her immigration status. He took the rap. He actually was guilty. He'd beat the living shit out of the fat bastard who'd laid hands on Evita. He was no slouch in a fight.

Found guilty and carted off to prison, Talco learned real quick who his true friends were. Evita was the only one who stuck with him when the chips were down. It was her money he spent on a shyster attorney who did little if anything for his defense. Evita was a keeper. He married her two days after his release from serving twelve months, a two year suspended sentence hanging over his head. She'd waited the entire year without complaint. She was there when no one else gave a damn. She'd proven her worth a hundred times over.

He owed it to Evita to keep a cool head. He swallowed down his pride and fury and tried reasoning with the detectives. "Hey, take it easy! I'll do what I can, but don't expect miracles. If my people know who she is, then we got her. I'm on it."

"Damn straight you are, and you're gonna pay the fuckin' tab too!" Oberman motioned to the waitress, "Hey, can I get another round over here?" Oberman and Konowicz always drank their fill when someone else was paying for it.

* * * *

CHAPTER 8

Awake in bed at sunset of the following evening, Michelle lying next to him, Aaron knew he needed to contact his roommate Kyle very soon. Besides, if it was Michelle's wish that he live with her, he needed to get his stuff from Kyle's place.

He couldn't imagine sleeping anywhere but her bed after the phenomenal sexual acrobatics of the night before—insanely erotic things he'd never imagined in his wildest fantasies. To top it all off, there was no fear of STD's or pregnancy. Another one of those fringe benefits of being vampires. Nothing but purely awesome, condom-free sex and a whole lot of biting.

The downside? He was now madly, irrevocably, undeniably, hooked on Michelle. It scared the crap out of him. His limited experience with serious relationships taught him one lesson very clearly. Women can destroy a man's peace and turn the whole world on its head in a matter of seconds. Michelle was no exception. If she ever got truly angry with him he'd be royally fucked.

Despite this fear and uncertainty, he couldn't ever recall having felt this strongly for another person. His relationship with Delia couldn't hold a candle to the intensity of emotional attachment he felt toward Michelle. His whole world revolved around Michelle. He could actually sense her thoughts, feelings and emotions, 24/7. In a way he was Michelle, and she him. It was becoming difficult to tell where her feelings ended and his began.

He wasn't sure how to bring it up without sounding like a lovesick puke. He decided to just go for it, put it out there and see what happens. He approached the subject of Kyle and his apartment cautiously. "Should I assume that I'm living here now, *permanently?*"

Michelle was engrossed in her iPhone, texting like mad. "*Oui.* Is necessary for the moment." She paused, sent another flurry of text flying through the airwaves, and continued, "I have a new job for you. I sent your pictures to the escort service and they like you. There are several women scheduling appointments to see you."

She has pictures of me? When were those taken? OMG—I hope I had clothes on. He opened his mouth to protest and thought better of it. It seemed prudent to say as little as possible when it came to Michelle. She already knew *way* too much about his thoughts and feelings.

"You have a date tomorrow night with an older woman who likes sexy, young boy toys. Five hundred dollars an hour. Is much better than strip clubs. The ladies, they pay you for the bite. Is *parfait*. Sex is not necessary, but maybe later, when you have learned control. One good bite with a happy ending is enough to satisfy. Is easy when they look you in the eyes, you have dominance. You lead with suggestion." Michelle dropped this bombshell in his lap without ceasing her flurry of text activity or one moment of eye contact.

"This we practice tonight. Remember to be *very* careful not to cause the addiction. Is very important!" There it was again, the veiled threat. She didn't quite say it, but he knew she was thinking it. Thinking about how she'd kill him if he proved uncontrollable.

"Is there a *problème*?" After seconds of stunned silence from him, she jumped up and pecked him on the cheek with her most sincere look of innocence. He was fast learning to regard that look with suspicion. It seemed her faux innocence became more convincing when she was up to something, like roping him into a job as a male escort.

He snapped back at her sarcastically, "No. No big problem. But don't you think you should ask before making plans on my behalf? I do have a job you know. I had a life before I met you."

She popped her head up to peg him with a stare that communicated her irritation. "This restaurant is no good for you. You must *sever* ties with those you knew before. You are very much changed now. People are not stupid. They notice the difference." She spoke with an air of impatience as though telling him something he should already know.

He scowled, his mind awhirl at the prospect of working as an escort in the sex trade. He knew escorts were rarely ever just an escort. It was nothing but a technically legal term for prostitution. Escort rolled off the tongue a little easier, but it still left a sour taste in his mouth.

She continued explaining that which he should have understood by now. "Is better we live the nightlife alone. No relations with friends or family. They are like *cattle*. We feed from them, but nothing more. Is a dangerous game to play. You will risk they learn the truth?" She surveyed him with the raised eyebrow of you-know-I'm right-and-you're-wrong.

He shook his head in denial of her truth.

"*Le prix à payer est lourd*. The price we pay for this life is obscurity. They can never know our true natures. We would be hunted. We take many pains to avoid this. No relationships with the food! It cannot be."

Her logic began to sink home.

He shook his head in resignation. "I suppose you're right. I should have seen this for myself. I guess I didn't think about it. It's probably best to break these connections now. I should go to my apartment, get my things, and give my roommate some excuse. Maybe I'll give him a bit of the truth. I'm living with you now, and I work with an escort service as eye candy for lonely, wealthy women." He was being sarcastic, but Michelle took him seriously.

"*Oui,* is a good idea. Tomorrow night. Tonight is more *training.* You still have much to learn."

And that was that, subject closed.

As they exited the apartment building, she laid her hand on his chest to stop him. "Wait for me here, *cher.*"

Ten minutes passed, and then ten more. He stood in the wet drizzle, on the sidewalk where she'd instructed him to wait. He waited, and waited some more. At the point he was ready to head back up and find out what the hell was keeping her, it happened.

"COME TO ME."

It hit him with a massive adrenaline surge. He needed to be there now, now, now. He darted into the alleyway, zinged past a stack of pallets and leaped over the five foot high dumpster in his way. In another second, he'd leaped up in the air snatching the metal railing of the fire escape. Up and over, and he was running. As his feet pounded out a rapid fire staccato beat up the metal stairs, his mind filled with the urgent need to get to Michelle on the roof. Within seconds he reached the top level catwalk of the fire escape, leaping to the edge of the roof, thirty feet above. With a desperate scrabble of hands and elbows he made it over the edge. She was right there, he could feel it. His vision zoomed in on her as he ran balls out to reach her.

He almost plowed right into her, barely skidding to a stop inches away. He felt an aggression he'd never known before, an urge to attack/defend. His enhanced senses ranged out over the roof top, seeking sounds, smells, or telepathic signature of some nameless threat. He felt primed for battle, a truly powerful and exhilarating experience.

Michelle congratulated him with a quirky, lopsided grin, "Very impressive! It only took you forty seconds to reach me. I'm very proud of you." She squeezed his biceps and kissed him on the lips as if he was the conquering hero welcomed home.

He huffed and panted heavily to catch his breath. "What was that all about?" His nerves were stretched taut, a bowstring ready to snap.

"Is a test to see how quickly you respond to my call. You passed beautifully. Is good exercise to learn coordination. You are faster and stronger than I am, you know?"

He had to admit she was right. He'd moved pretty damn fast. It was fucking *awesome*. He felt proud and powerful. Both feelings were quickly swamped by his rising irritation. Michelle had that effect on him regularly, an assault of mixed signals and emotions.

She touched him, holding his gaze without blinking while sending a strong sense of calm and approval. It hit like a tranquilizer, draining his aggression and relaxing the tension.

Realization soured his belly. This had been a convenient demonstration. She held the power to order him around, and then manipulate his feelings about it after the fact. He felt like the golden retriever living up to its namesake, retrieving the stick for its master. Michelle's behavior smacked of a prideful dog owner patting him on the head saying, *good boy*, while he stood there wagging his tail, waiting to play fetch all over again. As much as it bothered him, he couldn't shake that lingering sense of pride at her words of praise.

They returned to the street level with the same high-flying acrobatic maneuvers of the night before. Michelle stepped off the side of the building, and he followed right behind her, without even being asked. The difference now, as he followed Michelle downwards in the descending switch-back game, he moved with confidence and grace. He had begun to learn to coordinate his new strength and speed, and he had to confess he felt physically invincible. He couldn't really maintain a bitter attitude about Michelle's little training exercise. The game had served its purpose. He was flying high on his exhibition of masculine power. All other petty concerns became meaningless.

Rolling through the streets in a taxi, Michelle explained her plans. "We wait until one a.m., the clubs are now full. People are drunk." Her fingers slid over her his lap, teasing across the tip of his cock.

"We find the women dancing together. Is too easy. Feed quick. Thirty seconds, no more. You must learn to count. Is good exercise for control." She snapped her fingers. "Bite and move on to another girl." Her tongue licked her lips in a flicker. He sensed her excitement at having a hunting partner.

Upon entering the club, Michelle weaved through the crowd to the dance floor with Aaron in tow. She maneuvered them to a group of girls dancing together wedged into the center of the dance floor. Michelle and Aaron slipped into the middle of them swaying seductively to the music, maintaining constant eye contact.

He began to notice something different. These girls were watching him, and they were *interested*. Women didn't look at him that way. Not unless they were so drunk they looked at everyone that way. These girls wanted him. They moved in *closer*. Before he knew it, two girls sandwiched him and began grinding front to back. He'd never been singled out by two women for such intimate attentions. It was an incredible sensation to command the affections of several beautiful women.

He could get used to this real fast. Being the focus of so much attention was intoxicating. He felt like a rock star partying with his entourage in the VIP section. He looked over at his fellow rock-star-vampire-master. She was getting down to business.

While the ladies got funky, grinding all up on him, he gawked at Michelle in morbid fascination. She had already bit into one girl for a few seconds, and immediately turned towards another girl behind her for a second bite, making short work of anyone within reach. Nobody seemed to notice what he saw. They were being tapped one right after the other, all totally oblivious. She was an illusionist of the highest order, sleight of hand and fang. The cattle were blinded by her splendor.

The girl in front of Aaron leaned back into him with her backside, offering the juicy target of her neck and shoulder. She looked up with a seductive smile, giving him the eye contact he needed. Her petite, golden-brown Latina curves begged to be bitten. She licked her lips suggestively, an invitation he could hardly refuse. He struck hard and fast, letting the feeding instinct take over as he sunk into her exposed neck swallowing down her red, delicious life. The girl reached up to run her fingers through his hair, cupping his cheek in her palm.

"Mas, mas, don't stop!" She fisted her hand in his hair with her explosive orgasm.

He didn't want to let go. Every instinct in his body said to hold on, suck until there was nothing left to take. He dug down deep to find the strength of will to release her after what seemed like thirty seconds. He pulled back leaving her hot and bothered, unsatisfied. Reading her mind was a lesson in desire. She wanted more. She wanted him to do it again. She didn't have a clue what he'd done, but she wanted him to keep doing it. The girl smiled up at him with a drugged, dazed look, a light sheen of perspiration on her forehead, her dark iris faded to solid black from dilation. He had made a new friend.

Michelle flashed her eyes at him, sending a psychic kick through their mutual bond, silently urging him to move on. He turned away from the Latina to face a tall, willowy blonde who matched him in height. In seconds his unwavering eye contact gave him the control he needed. When he beckoned, she came. She moved right up on him, aligning her slim curves with his body as they both swayed to the music. She wore a short blue dress and easily straddled his thigh, spreading her legs to place her most intimate flesh on his leg, her hips grinding in time with the music. The Latina behind refused to be dismissed so easily. Latina began working to regain his attention. She molded herself to his backside with her arms flowing around him, slipping her fingertips into the front waistband of his pants.

He bit down straight into the pulse of the blonde grinding her moist sex on his leg. He tried his best to focus on only one girl at a time, even though they both struggled to gain his attention. Within seconds the blonde took his hand in hers, pulling his fingers down, inviting him to touch where she needed him most. Her dress had hiked up exposing her inner thighs to his caress. While he drank deeply, she used his hand to massage her swollen wet cunt, leaking her wetness onto his fingers.

The Latina hadn't given up the battle for Aaron's affections—she worked *harder* to regain his attention. With her hand down the front of his pants, she tugged his cock to a full-blown erection. He was so drunk on the overlapping sensations of blood and seduction that he almost fed too long from the blonde. As he released her neck, she became more aggressive with her ministrations, pulling her underwear aside to shove his fingers partway into her slippery wet warmth. At the same time, the Latina spooning him from behind worked him harder, faster, a skilled hand.

For the second night in a row, Michelle abruptly cut into his erotic fun when she grabbed his free arm and yanked him out of the clutches of the sex sandwich. She plowed through the wall-to-wall dancers with Aaron in tow. He looked over his shoulder to see two disappointed faces scowling at him.

When they reached the exit, Michelle turned to him with a sly smile. "Sorry to interrupt, but this was out of control. You did very well with timing, but you must not engage them sexually in public. You attract the wrong kind of attention. You don't want the attention of security and police." She smooched him on the cheek and led him outside to the taxi. She didn't seem angry. In fact she appeared aroused. Her eyes dilated with pleasure.

"Your eye contact gives you control, especially when they are drunk. Arousal from the bite and your natural attraction will drive women to rape you in public. Is a sexual frenzy. You must learn to moderate your effect." She was stroking his arm and crotch seductively. A study in contradictions—to speak of moderation while arousing him to the point of explosion.

"I know is difficult. Is very exciting. Even to me, just watching you is exciting. I will take good care of you tonight." She punctuated the promise by gripping his erection with her hand down his pants while kissing him.

This new life with Michelle? *Well, pretty damn cool so far.* He hoped that someday her affections might become genuine, something more than desire and lust. He wished that one day soon she could feel as strongly about him as he felt about her.

* * * *

CHAPTER 9

Aaron had mentally prepared himself for a quick in-and-out meeting with Kyle. He felt confident he could explain away having disappeared for almost a week.

Michelle blew his carefully constructed plans all to hell. "Let's go. Is time to close the door to your previous life. We must see this friend of yours."

He knew there was a good chance they might run into Delia and her friends there as well. *This is gonna be a disaster.* Like watching the cars pile up one by one in a train wreck; he saw it coming from a mile away.

"I don't know if it's such a good idea to bring you along. Things might get complicated. My ex-girlfriend could be there. Maybe it would be better if I do this alone." He gave it his best shot at diplomacy, but he already knew from his connection to her thoughts and feelings, Michelle would not be deterred.

"I will make certain is very clear to your friends that you are mine!"

It felt good to hear her declare something so intimate, but her manner made him uneasy.

"You will take us now to see your friends." Spoken in the unmistakable timbre of command, Michelle ceased all debate on the matter.

* * * *

"Hey guys, how's it going? I just stopped by for a few minutes to say hi. I'm in a hurry. Gotta run." Aaron edged in the front door, hoping not to attract too much attention. He prayed that he could get in and out quickly.

Kyle popped his head out the bedroom door near Aaron with a surprised look. Delia and her two friends stood at the far side of the room deep in conversation. The girls were debating the usual meaningless drivel of he said/she said. They hadn't noticed Aaron yet, but Kyle was quick on the draw.

"Whoa dude, where the hell have you been? I called your cell like thirty times. I was beginning to think you were dead!" Kyle was all over him with a suspicious look on his face. Aaron read his thoughts, which were even more suspicious than his face revealed: "*Where has he been? What the fuck was he thinking? How are we gonna pay the rent if he lost his job? Why didn't he answer any of my calls? Oh shit, who is this magnificent piece of ass wrapped around him? OH. My. God! She's a fuckin' knockout!*"

Michelle most definitely fit the description of *a fuckin' knock out*. She was dressed in a tight-fitted pink top with dark blue jeans that molded to every delicious curve of her body. *Painted on.*

Aaron had to check himself. He almost answered questions Kyle hadn't spoken aloud.

He caught himself at the last second. "This is my ... *friend* ... Michelle. Michelle, this is my roommate Kyle." He hadn't known what word to use to describe her. *Friend* was the only thing that came to mind that would make any sense to Kyle. Referring to her as his *Vampire Master* probably wouldn't work out so well.

As he spoke, Aaron looked at Michelle several times. Her demeanor had magically transformed into the *sexy-girl-next-door*. She clung to his arm as if they'd known each other all their lives. Nothing short of miraculous. She could be quite the actress when she needed to. She held his eyes for a moment. He caught a mischievous twinkle in her eye. The real Michelle was still lurking in there waiting to pounce.

"*Bonjour,* everyone, is nice to meet you. And you too, Kyle. Aaron has told me so much about you. I feel as though I already know you." He followed Kyle's mind as he spun off in speculation of what Aaron might have said about him.

He had to placate Kyle's unanswered questions quietly before the rest of the room got involved in the conversation. Delia and crew stared in their direction.

"Listen man, I've been *staying* with Michelle the past week. I'm really sorry I didn't call you." Aaron leaned into Kyle, speaking quietly in a conspiracy of two men appreciating the obvious good fortune of spending a week in Michelle's bed.

"Really, I'm sorry. I lost my cell phone, and then I met Michelle, and it's been totally crazy. But it's all good, you know." Reading his mind, Kyle tried to envision Aaron on a bender, partying it up with Michelle. Didn't make sense to Kyle, Aaron's personality didn't allow for such behavior.

Delia and company closed in from across the room. He tried to be fast and discrete. "Seriously, Michelle is *so* awesome. She has this fantastic apartment and I got a new job that pays way better than Bemichis. I'm moving in with Michelle."

Kyle popped at this last statement. Aaron realized from the course of Kyle's thoughts that he'd neglected to address the primary concern, *the rent.*

Kyle started in on him. "Hey, man, you're moving pretty fast here. I mean we have rent coming due in a couple of days and … um … you two barely met!" Kyle had begun to panic. He could see from his thoughts that Kyle actually didn't have enough to pay the rent on his own.

Delia and gang surrounded Aaron. They had gathered the basic concept that he was moving out of Kyle's apartment and in with the blonde goddess caressing his arm. Aaron glanced at Delia briefly. She looked different now. He didn't see all those adorable little details that had once fascinated him, holding him in a constant state of frustrated arousal. Delia's shoulder-length, dirty blonde hair didn't shine like it used to. Her cute, little sassy look now appeared spiteful and catty. Seeing her now was like looking at an old photograph, remembering something long forgotten. Delia seemed *diminished,* less than. She couldn't begin to measure up to Michelle.

As Delia and her two friends moved into flanking positions, blocking off avenues of retreat, Michelle intervened. She addressed Kyle as though he'd been speaking to her with his protests. "*Oui,* is true, we just met a few days ago. But what can I say? Is *très magnifique!* We are together all the time. Is like I don't want to let him escape!"

He snickered. *If only they knew how very true those words are.*

With this, Michelle reached around and squeezed his ass, planting a loud smooch on his cheek. He was now marked territory with a big sign hanging from his rear that said, *Property of Michelle—NO TRESPASSING.*

Delia looked both Aaron and Michelle up and down with a scowl painted on her face. He read how Delia puzzled over what qualities he had that could attract Michelle and keep her occupied for an entire week. Delia wondered if she'd missed out on something. Maybe she should've let Aaron have his way with her. Was he really *all that* in bed? She thought perhaps he was like that guy from the movie *Fight Club*—an unremarkable, scrawny weasel who suddenly transforms into a badass alter-ego, a screw-your-brains-out-all-night-long Brad Pitt.

Aaron became overwhelmed at the girls' thoughts in response to Michelle's boldness. All three girls and Kyle hit his mind in a tumbled mess of irritated confusion. "*What is she saying? Are they sleeping together? Is he living with her now? God, I wish I had her hair. What a slut! I bet she has him totally pussy-whipped. That's so typical of Aaron to fall in love with the first girl who grabs his ass. Look at her eyes. That color is freakish, that's gotta be contacts. Those are seven hundred dollar Gucci shoes! I bet he paid her to do this. She can't be for real. What could she possibly see in him? Delia must be dying with jealousy by now!*"

Dazed and confused, Michelle tugged on his arm, bringing him out of his internal mess.

"Is only fair to Kyle we pay this month's rent. Is so sudden." Michelle had entranced Kyle. He was putty in her hands as she maintained her wicked soul-snatching eye contact. The woman could charm the skin off a king cobra. Her distraction provided Aaron the stimulus he needed to hastily erect a mental block to ward off the tangled assault of thoughts aimed in his direction.

After enjoying a couple seconds of mental silence, he got with the program. "Yeah, um … I guess you're right." He turned to Kyle and offered a wad of bills that Michelle had given him the night before. "Here's six hundred. That should cover you through the next month."

Kyle nodded in agreement with a dreamy, idiotic expression. He barely managed a one word answer, "Okay."

As Kyle shoved the cash into his pants pocket in a crumpled ball, Michelle finalized the transaction with one of her adorable French asides. "*Viola!*"

This foreign sound from Michelle elicited frowns from all three girls. Kyle remained bewitched with his idiot smile pasted on. Amber, the girl to the right of Delia, leaned in, looking back and forth at Aaron and Michelle. "Wow, that's really cool. So like … you guys are moving in together?"

As she spoke, Amber nudged Delia with her elbow. Delia barely noticed. She stared unwaveringly at Aaron.

He made the mistake of staring back, catching Delia directly in the eyes with the full force of his gaze. He forgot how powerful his eye contact could be. He broke away from her stare after a few seconds, but the damage was done. He followed her thoughts as Delia picked up on the subtle but distinct differences in her ex-boyfriend. She felt a near irresistible attraction to him, far stronger than ever before. She wanted to run her hands all over him, under his shirt, down his pants. There was something disturbing about him, something strange, almost unnatural. She regretted having dumped him two weeks ago. This situation wasn't right at all. Aaron had always been hers, wrapped around her little finger.

Delia began to realize she might have been wrong. Aaron was a real catch after all. What had she been thinking when she broke up with him? Aaron wasn't supposed to go off dating European models. He was supposed to be jealous, begging her to take him back.

He frowned as he recalled doing just that. She had him groveling, calling her several times a day, leaving syrupy voicemails and text messages on her cell for an entire week. Right up to the moment he met Michelle.

Listening to Delia's thoughts gave him inspiration. "Michelle, this is Delia. She's a *friend* of mine. Delia, meet my *girlfriend*, Michelle." Delia flinched as though physically stung by the intensity of Michelle's scrutiny as she looked her up and down.

Michelle gave him the opening he needed. "Why don't you get your things while I gossip about you with your friends?"

What goes around comes around, Delia. Off the hook, he headed for his bedroom mumbling, "Good idea."

* * * *

Delia moved toward Aaron to follow him. She was halted in her tracks by Michelle's firm grasp on her arm. She turned to Michelle with a blatant sneer, and was immediately captured by those vivid green eyes in an intense staring contest.

"I know you were with him before, but I hope we can be friends. These things can sometimes be a *problème, non?*" She still had an iron grip on Delia's arm, staring directly into her eyes without blinking.

The spell finally broke. Delia shook her head and stammered, "No … um … I mean … no problem. I … we broke it off weeks ago. It's cool. He's … we're just friends now. Are you guys, like … dating?"

Delia hadn't fooled anyone. Her tension was obvious despite her attempts to appear calm. She displayed her nervous tick, pulling a stray hair behind her ear, avoiding further eye contact with Michelle. Delia looked to her friends for support. Amber jumped to her aid.

"Oh yeah, it's alright. They broke up, like, two weeks ago. It's all good."

Delia bobbed her head. Amber joined in, both nodding emphatically, a united front declaring Aaron to be a free man. They wouldn't dare think of laying their hands on him. Michelle could have him all to herself, no problem at all. No one who knew Delia was fooled, and neither was Michelle.

Kyle had enough of this drama. He addressed Michelle. "So, you live here in New York? How long have you been here?" Their conversation delved into the safe platonic zones of weather, traffic, and the rudeness of New York taxi drivers.

* * * *

Aaron made sure to stay busy in his room, away from all the stares and pointed thoughts. As he assessed his possessions and stuffed them into a couple trash bags he realized just how much his world had changed in the span of one week. He no longer felt any attachment to this *place*, these *people*, or his *stuff*. His meager clothing appeared drab and unsuited to his new personality and life style. His books and music no longer interested him. His friends in the other room, ensorcelled by his vampire master, no longer held any emotional significance for him. By comparison to the radiant Michelle, Delia was a self-absorbed, frumpy, awkward little girl, who was now uninteresting and frankly irritating. He couldn't remember what it was about her that had appealed to him in the first place.

He recalled his life in this bedroom as it had revolved around Delia and Kyle. The memory in his mind's eye seemed like a lifetime ago. A life lived by a different Aaron. He recalled passing his days between work, partying with Kyle, and the foolish pursuit of Delia's paltry affections. His life had reached a significant fork in the road. The instant he aligned paths with Michelle there was no turning back. Every night traveled down this new path took him that much farther away from humanity.

He quickly finished gathering his junk and prepared to leave. He overheard Michelle dropping the "E" bomb as he walked out of his room.

"Aaron is working with me now in the *Escort Service*. Here is my card with my cellular. Aaron's cards will be ready in a few days, you can reach him at my cell."

Thoughts exploded left and right, front, side, and back. The mental shrapnel hit Aaron every which way. He took deep, calming breaths as he scrunched up his eyes in concentration to block out the pummeling assault focused on him: *"She's an Escort! She's a prostitute! She's pimping Aaron out! They must be junkies! She's got him strung out on crack! He's lost his mind! I knew she wasn't with him for real. It's a business transaction! God, I wonder how much she charges per hour? Could I afford a half-hour, catch a friendly discount? Maybe just a blow job?"*

He did his best to get a grip, slowly and methodically shielding the waspish buzz of thoughts directed at him. Michelle grabbed his hand, lending him her calming influence and strength.

She setup a fast exit. "Ah ... you are ready? Sorry to run, but we have things to do and people to see. Very nice to meet you all. *Adieu!*"

He took full advantage of the moment. "Bye guys. Talk to you later. I'll see you around. Take care." They were all staring, jaws agape from shock. None of them dared to say what they were thinking. Kyle couldn't stop imagining what it would be like to get a half-hour freebie from Michelle. He kept picturing her going down on him, her blonde hair bobbing back and forth as she sucked him off.

Aaron jetted for the door. There was nothing to be gained by spending another second in the presence of these *humans*.

As he turned his back on his former life, Michelle couldn't resist one last jab. "Your friends were *so* nice to me. I'm glad we met." She snatched a handful of his ass and nailed all four of them with the silent message in a backward glance over her shoulder.

They closed the door behind them with Kyle yelling, "Don't be a stranger." But Aaron knew things would never be the same again, because he was already a stranger.

On the taxi ride back to Michelle's apartment he pondered if Michelle's show of possessiveness was simply an attempt to help navigate the situation with Kyle and Delia, or if there might be the slightest hint of real affection.

* * * *

CHAPTER 10

Aaron's spirits soared, he had made his escape from Kyle and Delia relatively unscathed. He'd been nervous about the situation, but was pleasantly surprised at how easily Michelle handled *the gang*. She was quite charming, a nice change from her aggressive control freak persona.

After dropping off Aaron's trash bags full of stuff at Michelle's apartment they headed out again to another nightclub where Michelle knew the doorman personally. Her connection ushered them through the door immediately. They made a bee line for the dance floor and located a group of girls huddled together in a tightly-packed formation. Picking through the brains of the nearby girls, digging for those who were attracted to him, he found they all had one thing in common. Though each girl was different, each mind having its own particular *flavor*, a mutual desire was prevalent throughout the crowd. All these women really wanted was to meet a man—not just any man—a man who might be *the one*.

He thought it funny how these women went out with their friends hoping to be romanced off their feet as they dance the night away with that special man. The reality more often than not was ridiculous. The ladies stayed securely locked away in their *safe zone* with their girlfriends, brushing away the majority of the men who would chance to meet them. These girls discouraged and actively worked against the very thing they desired most, a meaningful romantic encounter. They wouldn't find what they were looking for with Aaron, but they never stopped hoping. The women who noticed Aaron viewed him as a target for acquisition—a good candidate—never once seeing past the charming boyish exterior to the underlying truth. He was there to feed upon the *cattle*. Damn lucky a little nip was all he planned on taking. It would be too easy to take anything he wanted.

The vampires slid through the crush of swaying bodies like snakes in the tall grass. Their prey couldn't see them coming until it was too late. The girls were no match for the animal magnetism radiated by the hunting vampires. As they selected targets one at a time, the unsuspecting girls thought themselves the chosen elite, excited to be singled out from the crowd by one of these sublimely beautiful creatures. Instead of fearing their proximity to a predator, they felt privileged to receive the attentions of either Aaron or Michelle.

He had begun to discern a pattern. It was always this way with the cattle. They were completely unaware of the danger. Was it his benign intentions putting them at ease? What excuse might there be for Michelle? She could never be categorized as *benign*. This was definitely a rapacious pursuit on her part. The only rationale that seemed to fit was ignorance. They honestly did not perceive the threat in their midst. The vampires were able to feed upon the women one at a time without a single member of the herd ever realizing they'd been singled out for attack. They didn't know what was happening right before their eyes on the dance floor.

Each girl they encountered was enthralled, bitten, thoroughly dowsed with sexual ecstasy and then discarded as the vampires moved on to the next target. It seemed as though they lined up for it, eagerly awaiting their turn like children with the ice-cream man. The attraction they exuded was the ice-cream truck musical tune, signaling to come and get it, one and all. Enough to go around. He felt like he could do this all night long, feeding from one woman after another. His thirst was insatiable. The thirty-second nips they snagged here and there only took the edge off.

By the time Michelle finished, he had hit full swing, having fed from six different girls and ready to take on another dozen. She tried to reason with him.

"That is more than enough for now. We must go before we attract the attention of security. They are beginning to notice." She gave him a mental nudge in the direction of a massive bald black guy with a black t-shirt that said *SECURITY*. She was right; the man eyed them suspiciously. When Aaron focused on the security guard's thoughts, he realized the guy suspected they might be pickpockets from the way they worked the room.

Despite the obvious threat from security, Aaron's bloodlust was kickin'. He wanted to feed more. Now. He didn't give a shit what the big scary man thought of him. Three girls nearby had eyes for him, wishing he'd come talk to them. He had every intention of doing so. The new and improved Aaron Pilan was not easily intimidated by *humans*, even if they weighed three hundred plus pounds.

Michelle glared at him issuing a none-too-subtle command, "We Go Now!"

And that was that.

He followed Michelle out the exit, his movements jerky and mechanical like a marionette. Her marching orders went against every instinct in his body. What he really desired more than anything was to feed. He didn't want to leave. He wanted to set up camp in that nightclub, hang out all night long––till sunrise—tasting every single woman who walked in the door.

Maybe another nightclub? He opened his mouth to make the suggestion. She stopped him with her fingers on his lips and "the look." The I-already-know-what-you're-gonna-say-and-the-answer-is-NO, look.

He didn't bother asking.

In the taxi ride home, Michelle surprised him by reaching down into the front of his designer DKNY black slacks. She freed his semi-hard cock from his pants and promptly went down on him. It only took her a few seconds to suck him to full-tilt rock hardness. She sucked and sucked and sucked until thoughts of feeding and bloodlust were replaced with another kind of desire.

"Oh shit. Damn!"

She grunted and slurped, making wet guttural sounds as she swallowed him whole over and over. She pulled and tugged, stroked and sucked, until he couldn't think or move except to grip the armrest for dear life as he was rocked by the force of his release into her powerful warm suction.

The taxi driver tactfully looked the other way with a grin he couldn't hide as Michelle slipped Aaron's spent manhood back into his pants. She zipped him up and tucked his shirt back in like a mother primping her child to send him off to school. She patted his thigh affectionately, smiled as she wiped her mouth with a tissue, and licked her lips in a silent promise of good things to come. He wondered how hard he'd have to scrub to remove all that red lipstick from his groin.

He was struck with a lightning bolt realization—he loved her so much it hurt. She was everything to him: his mother, goddess, lover, caretaker, and the most gorgeous and sexiest woman he had ever known.

She ruined the magic of the moment when she started asking questions.

"Are there any more friends or family we need to deal with? What of your parents? Why don't you speak of them?"

* * * *

Michelle sensed her probing had struck a nerve. This was a sensitive issue for Aaron.

He gave her a non-answer. "I don't really have any other friends I hang out with. And my parents ... well ... there's nothing to say there. My father died and I don't really speak with my mother much anymore."

She didn't like the potential loose ends of Aaron's former life still out there blowing in the breeze. She needed to be certain there wouldn't be any surprises from his past rearing their ugly head in her nicely-ordered existence. She enjoyed the simplicity of detachment from humanity. A lonely life, but one without complications. Michelle had learned the hard way, through costly mistakes, that she could not build or maintain relationships with *people*. They were food and entertainment, nothing more. In her experience, these affairs always ended to the detriment or death of her human companions.

She briefly considered ordering him to talk. She could force his hand, but that seemed extreme and unjustified. She knew how it felt to be on the receiving end of compulsive authority. She was acutely aware of the fine line between control and abuse in relation to Aaron's free will.

Perhaps another form of coercion would be better for making him talk. Having decided upon a course of action, she didn't hesitate. She continued rubbing his thighs, reaching inward to tease his cock back into semi-hardness. She barely let up as they exited the taxi into the apartment building, caressing and kissing him in the elevator.

She tortured him delicately, watching him squirm as his eyes rolled back in his head with her sensuous massage. His cock stiffened out straight in his pants. Upon entering the apartment, he hurriedly stripped his clothes. She backed off, smirking. He stood naked before her, his raging erection pointing in accusation as if to say, *you did this to me.*

She studied him, appreciating her handiwork, pleased with his display. She stepped up, taking him firmly in hand, and whispered, "Please tell me. I want to know. Tell me of your parents. I don't like secrets."

As she spoke, her fingers slid down the length of him to his most vulnerable point. She cupped him, his precious jewels safely ensconced in her tender grip. Her hands and fingers kept moving slowly, sliding and testing his size and weight.

She stroked all that soft, yet hard cock. His mindless arousal rolled off his aura in waves. She had stolen away all reason with skilled, calculated seduction. His thoughts broadcast to her loud and clear. He wanted to throw her on the floor and ravage her body. Nothing else existed in his world beyond the need to be inside her, to finish what she started.

Using both hands now, while kissing his ears and neck, she continued to work him without mercy, stroking his full velvet shaft and his taut balls. She whispered again in his ear, brushing her lips across his skin lightly, her tongue flickering in his ear. "You promise to tell me everything after we finish?"

His powerful arousal had sparked her own. Her panties were soaked through with anticipation. It was all she could do to continue the game, holding his explosion at bay.

She knew the poor boy was so drunk on lust he would have agreed to assassinate the president if asked. His whole essence was consumed by the unbearable need to be buried inside her. He answered without reservation. "Yes, Michelle, I promise!"

With his agreement, she flung off her clothes, stripping pants, top, and underwear in a lightning-fast blurred Superman-in-the-telephone-booth frenzy. She emerged from the whirlwind stripper routine completely naked. She leaped at him ferociously and pinned him against the wall. His hands gripped her ass, and he shoved all that hard cock straight up into her.

"Dieu qui fait mal!" God that hurts!

And he definitely didn't slow down on her account. He slammed into her over and over, his claws digging into her ass painfully. He hit home, right where she had taught him to go, hitting that spot. It was so rare a man knew where to give it to her. She pumped her hips to keep up with his sexual assault, riding his wave.

"Oh shit! Yes!" he cried out as he pounded her with every inch he had to give.

In the maelstrom of sensations, their psyches merged to become one, each knowing how to accommodate the other. He pumped hard and fast, slamming home to her limit as she ground her hips with animal grunts and squeals. It actually hurt quite a bit, he was so powerful. But it was the *right* kind of hurt.

They growled and grunted their way to an explosive climax, biting deep and hard simultaneously. Their psychic bond synced them perfectly. They knew where, when, and how to pleasure themselves, and they knew exactly when and where to bite.

She kept at it, riding him upright with his back to the wall. She sunk her claws into the sheetrock of the wall while he pummeled her, his slamming thrusts bouncing her up into the air.

"Michelle!"

"Aaron!"

They growled each other's names as they both came hard. Sex, blood, pleasure and pain created a wicked lovely blend like no other experience in this world. She bit him over and over, keeping him hard and virile throughout their sexual marathon.

"Oh. *Oui, encore! Encore!*" She drove him mad, frenzied with her demands for more.

They continued pounding and grinding, destroying the living room wall in their fervor. When the post-orgasmic exhaustion hit, by tacit agreement through their psychic bond, they released their bites and gave it a rest. She collapsed in his arms, wrapped around him, his cock still shoved deep to her core. She didn't want to admit how wonderful it felt to have the unconditional love and attention of a powerful male vampire with his arms wrapped protectively around her. She could never connect with any other this way. Only with her own kind could it be so.

Why didn't I do this decades ago?

He carried her to the bed and laid his weight into her without separating. She could sleep with his cock buried in her all day long and know she'd never be alone again.

* * * *

It felt so damn wonderful inside Michelle. He wanted to stay there for the rest of the night. As she looked into his eyes, he thought he saw a look of heady emotion, something reminiscent of the way he felt for her. Michelle quickly masked her features with a dreamy smile of contentment. She boosted his ego off the charts when she admitted, "It hasn't been this good in a very long time."

She popped her hips, digging him in deeper, which he took as the signal to give it to her again. His zeal renewed with her admission. He pushed in harder and deeper, grinding down in to hit her where it hurt, where she liked it to hurt. Each thrust squeezed a sexy little noise from her lips, driving him crazy.

After another exhausting round of biting and orgasms, he settled down to hold her tightly, spooned from behind with his abused cock fit between her perfectly rounded ass cheeks and his mouth up against her ear. He could picture staying like this, with Michelle molded to his body, for eternity. The only reason he need move was to make love to her over and over again, and then return to this very same embrace afterwards. What a perfectly wonderful life, lying in bed with Michelle, screwing like rabbits. This was as good as it got.

* * * *

CHAPTER 11

They lay there for a time in the wonderful, magic afterglow of awesome sex, Michelle spooned up against Aaron. They were a good fit, his build seemed to match her, just right. She hated to do it and almost didn't, but she needed to know. She needed to be certain he was truly hers with no strings attached to his former life. She interrupted their beautiful moment of peace.

"*Mon chéri*, I am waiting patiently to hear your story. Tell me."

She caught the smile splitting his face, he knew her well enough to understand the limits of her patience had been reached. Then he laughed out loud, at her.

She flipped around to face him, her ferocity barely contained. She stared him down, daring him to break his promise. Though a smartass, she read his sense of obligation to keep his promise even though she'd extorted it from him at a moment of vulnerability.

"Okay ... um ... ... My father died ... six years ago. It was probably the worst time of my life." A searing avalanche of his pain accompanied his words. His grief burned all the way through their psychic bond. She sat up, shying away, trying to shut down their connection. No one should have to share that kind of pain, so intense, so personal.

It was pointless. She had stirred it up, and now the only thing to do was accept his pain, ride it out to the other side.

After a moment of shock and a couple quick gasps, she dived into his pain headfirst. She wrapped her arms around his waist to hug him close. She had forced the issue, at the very least she could offer some meager comfort.

He instantly calmed under her embrace. And then his mind opened wide to her as he spoke. She could actually feel and experience his memories; far more depth of imagery and emotion than could ever be communicated by speech alone. She flowed down into the pain-filled recesses of his memories––to the time of his father's funeral and an overwhelming sense of loss and grief. The pain was still there, strong as ever, suffocating. She felt her own throat constrict with it. A pain she understood well, the loss of a father. She couldn't help but think of her own father, in a time and place long removed from here. Her memory still carried its share of pain. *Perhaps it's something you never really get over. You just learn to live with it.*

His memories were most painful at the wake, standing in front of his father's coffin. Aaron didn't want to see the corpse in that shiny box, all painted up by a mortuary makeup artist who'd never known his father in life. That wasn't his father lying there, but the image branded into his memory. He couldn't rid himself of the memory. Aaron turned away quickly, preferring to look at the collage assembled by the entry to the chapel. The collage held a much truer representation of his father, not that dead thing in a box. He spent a good amount of time staring at the photographs, trying to overwrite the painted corpse image.

Michelle immediately noticed the telltale signs of family resemblance. Aaron had his father's smile and other small details like the shape of his jawline and set of his shoulders. She recognized something in his father's face, a solemnity, a quiet strength that she'd seen glimpses of from time to time in Aaron's demeanor. The kind of strength one doesn't see at first. A subtle quality.

Some of the pictures sparked corresponding memories of the times and places they were taken. A picture of Aaron in his early teens sitting next to his father holding up a fish triggered the memory of his father's voice urging him on. His father, Lucas Pilan, *Luke*, encouraged him. "Give her a fight. Don't let up. Keep the rod solid in your hand. Pull back, steady … steady … reel her in, slow and easy." Aaron was so excited and yet afraid to lose the fish. He didn't even like fish, but he wanted this one for his dad, who loved a good pan-fried trout with beer batter.

Focus shifted to another picture of his father in a hospital bed, looking embarrassed but still smiling. Aaron recalled how his dad maintained his good humor to the very end, even as the chemotherapy treatments and medications brought on recurring bouts of nausea, making him so tired that he slept through most of the day. Though his body was frail, Luke's spirit held strong. He'd smiled and laughed constantly, as if the discomfort was merely a distraction. At times his father would say, "I'm catching an early retirement out of this one … don't you worry, it's no big deal. You can't keep a good man down." He'd spout off ridiculous things like this while bedridden, in extreme pain. Aaron had often wondered if it was the pain meds talking, or his father trying to smooth it over, keeping up appearances for his family, or perhaps lying to himself.

Aaron recalled his problems in school. How he was held back in the tenth grade to repeat the year because he'd spent so much time with his father in the hospital. And then, again, he missed an entire month of school after his father had died. Ironically it wasn't the cancer that killed his dad, but the complications of internal bleeding after removing the tumor in surgery.

Another photo in the collage was Aaron at sixteen, just before his father's diagnosis of cancer. He sat with both parents at his birthday party; all three of them smiling with faces pressed together side by side and cheek to cheek. Aaron's mother, Angela, was a slight woman of dark brown hair, so dark, almost black, and sad brown eyes. Aaron obviously inherited something of Angela's cheek bones and the sad tilt of her eyes. They seemed happy. An average American family living day by day, blissfully unaware of how death would irrevocably change their lives, robbing Aaron of all his joy for years to come.

And then his mother had changed in the blink of an eye. Almost overnight his mother had disappeared, replaced with a complete stranger. She began dating all different kinds of men her friends introduced her to. She never warned Aaron of her intentions. She just did it. The extent to which she had consulted Aaron about her desire to date and move on with her life had been an off-hand comment about how *they both had to go on their lives* and *Luke wouldn't have wanted them to be lonely*. Before he knew it, she was out on Friday or Saturday nights until two-three-four in the morning. Sometimes she didn't bother coming home till the next day. Angela's behavior immediately after his father's death seemed a horrible betrayal of everything he held sacred.

They grew distant quickly. Aaron wasn't assertive enough to let her know how he felt. Long accustomed to the quiet, unobtrusive temperaments of both Aaron and his father, Angela didn't bother to ask what Aaron thought. Had she asked, it would've been purely courtesy. Angela Pilan had been bowling over her boys for years. She'd always found a way to get exactly what she wanted. Luke hadn't been the kind of man to set limits or argue with his wife. The Pilan men are long-suffering. Luke had been happy just to have Angela in his life. He taught Aaron to go with the flow when it came to the whims of his mother.

In going with the flow, Aaron withdrew from Angela. He found solace in his friends, Kyle and a couple other buddies. His grand plans for college and career were shelved for the day to day life of pursuing girls and enjoying the teen social scene of parties, movies, and music. It worked. Kept his mind off things at home he'd rather not deal with. Aaron stopped talking to his mother about anything he thought or felt. About anything at all. She didn't seem to notice. Or perhaps she preferred it that way. She never tried to reconnect with her son. Angela pursued the single's lifestyle, and Aaron took care of himself, rarely requiring anything from her.

Angela was busy making up for lost time, meeting new people, making new friends, and jumping from boyfriend to boyfriend almost monthly. During their family years, when Luke was still alive, Angela had maintained the habit of going to the local Catholic Church on Sundays. After his death, all pretenses were dropped. Aaron wondered that maybe he'd never truly known his mother all these years. It was as if she'd been maintaining appearances for Luke's sake, and now the real Angela showed her face for the first time.

As he spent more and more time hanging out with Kyle, making plans to get their own apartment, it seemed the life he'd once known with a mother and a father was something experienced in a dream.

The final episode between him and this woman Angela, this stranger he called mother, happened the day he met Charles Miller. An insurance salesman, Charles and Angela had hooked up three months prior. Somewhere during these three months, in which Aaron hadn't known the man existed, Charles and Angela had fallen in love and decided to marry.

This day was crisp and clear in Aaron's mind, branded and labeled as the day he lost whatever remaining sliver of the mother Angela had once been to this stranger, Charles. The man showed up at the house—the first time Aaron had ever seen him. Aaron realized right away his mother was serious about her relationship with Charles.

He gave it an honest effort to talk with Charles, to accept him into his life. Aaron's limited conversations with the man ranged over sports and religion, subjects on which Aaron had little comment or interest. Apparently, Angela had been miraculously restored in her faith by the divine hand of Charles Miller. All the two of them ever did was preach Jesus and salvation. Aaron couldn't run the opposite direction fast enough. It was painfully obvious they had no common ground to converse or build a relationship. As it turned out, it wasn't necessary for Aaron to welcome Charles into their home.

After meeting Charles, and sharing a meal together as though they were now a family, this strange woman inhabiting his mother's body pulled Aaron aside to talk with him privately. She told him *you're nineteen years old*, and *its time you moved out and became an adult*, and that *she wanted to live her life with Charles* without *the weirdness of another male adult in the household*. Aaron had listened to her in a daze of shock, simply nodding at the proper moments to indicate understanding. Understanding was the furthest thing from his mind on this day. He didn't get it at all. Where was his mother? Had she been invaded by body snatchers? Had she become one of those pod people? Who was this woman telling him to leave the only home he'd ever known? How could she toss him out on the street like the spring-cleaning trash?

He didn't recall if he had spoken to Angela beyond his dumbstruck nods of acknowledgement. He was too numbed with shock. He packed his clothes and stuff and moved into Kyle's apartment that very evening. When asked about it by Kyle and friends, Aaron answered simply, "It's the right time."

Until this very moment, lying in bed with Michelle's glorious naked body wrapped around him, Aaron never had a reason to look back on the past. It wasn't necessary.

Delia had never cared about Aaron's past, and Kyle had seemed to understand in a silent agreement that there was nothing to discuss regarding Aaron's mother. Aaron and Angela's relationship degenerated to the bare bones minimum of contact. He spoke to her on the required holidays in the American Christian custom. They exchanged gifts through the mail at Christmas and birthdays. Beyond that, neither one existed to the other.

Aaron kept on rolling forward, avoiding the need to think back and remember those bygone days when he'd once known what it was like to have a family. Those memories were too painful and always sparked resentment towards his mother. He blocked those memories away, trying his best to forget. There his memories stayed, buried in the riverbed of his life. He never found cause to dig into the soil and expose the past. It was easy for Aaron to fill the empty hours of his days with Kyle and Delia. As long as he kept busy, he had no time to brood on the past.

He lived his life cheerfully ignorant of the rest of the world outside Kyle and Delia until the day the world put Michelle in his path. Fate had gifted him—or cursed him—with this new turn of events. Aaron lay in bed holding the most beautiful woman in the world, bearing his soul through their mutual psychic bond, tears of blood streaming down his face from the remembrance of grief, pain and frustration he'd suppressed for years.

Michelle now knew everything about him: his past, his pain, his grief, his loneliness, and the little shoebox of a life he'd lived prior to meeting her. She was his confessional, his priest, his savior, his own personal Jesus Christ, laying his demons to rest with her touch, presence, and silent acceptance.

Purged of his sadness, allowing the memories to drift away to return to the vault of things better forgotten, Michelle agreed through silent psychic communication that this would never be spoken of again. Happy, limbs tangled together, they rested, content. She felt the satisfaction of problems resolved, demons conquered, and the comfort of a deeply rewarding connection. As dawn peeked over the horizon she drifted off to sleep like the dead in his embrace.

* * * *

CHAPTER 12

Talco pounded pavement for three nights straight, passing around the artist's rendering of the blonde tramp to every pimp, prostitute, and hustler he could find. Not one person recognized her. No one had ever seen or heard of her before. She'd never worked these streets, at least not anywhere near 60th and Palmetto.

He considered it a risk to speak with most of these people. Many of them were ex-cons. The rules of his probation forbid any contact with felons. It was completely absurd. How should he know if someone was a felon? Was he supposed to ask every person he met? "Hello, my name's Talco, oh ... by the way, are you a felon? I was just wondering because I'm on probation."

What an awesome way to make friends and influence people. How can a man get anywhere in life saddled with such ridiculous rules? In most cases he could tell whether or not a person had been to prison before by simply looking at them. But out on the streets? In the ghetto neighborhoods? Talco suspected his probation could get revoked simply for being in these areas. It looked way suspicious. And it made him extremely nervous.

This whole idea seemed stupid. Escorts and their dates don't find each other on street corners, it's foolish and suspicious, and a sure way to get tossed in jail. Girls didn't need to do that anymore. Not with free classified ad websites.

The more time he spent on this pointless, high risk activity, the more pissed off he became. He was certain she wasn't out walking these streets. So ... why was he beating the streets looking for this puta like a retard?

After three consecutive nights of wasted time he gave up. He'd have to find some other way to placate *Los Demonios*. Probably have to pay them off. The detectives certainly weren't giving him credit for his efforts without results. This was exactly what he'd been afraid of.

He had a wife and newborn baby at home who needed him. He definitely didn't need this shit. When he came home at midnight, Evita awaited him with a kiss and a smile, six month old Mateo held in the crook of her arm. They were the best thing that ever happened to him. He'd gained so much in so little time, but he stood to lose it all with this foolish business.

"What's wrong, baby? Que paso?" Evita smoothed away the tension from his forehead with her free hand, baby Mateo cooing quietly in her other arm.

She was so beautiful as a mother. She'd truly blossomed with Mateo's birth. Talco couldn't imagine life without her and his son. He knew if he went to prison again, Evita might not be there by the time he got out. There were only so many mistakes a girl would put up with. Her golden skin, spicy Colombian attitude, and beautiful hazel eyes would surely attract another man if Talco went down for too long. He had to find a way out of this mess. He had to stop chasing the easy money and go legit. He had to get away from those bastard detectives.

He answered Evita as he embraced her, "Todo está bien mi amor. I'm okay. You know I love you? Tu eres mi vida, mi corazón."

She had cooked his favorite dinner, fajitas Evita-style, with freshly prepared salsa and guacamole on the side. Beyond being the most gorgeous Colombian woman he'd ever met, she was also a damn good cook.

Evita Rodriguez, formerly Evita Valenzuela, had come to New York on a visa paid for by Colombian cartel, her stomach filled with tiny latex balloons of high purity cocaine. It was a fairly common way to catch a paid vacation to New York for Colombians who otherwise didn't have a dime to their name. She survived the ordeal without a single package bursting in her belly, collected her $5000 dollar payoff, and promptly disappeared into the streets of New York City.

Barely twenty when Talco met her, she began selling her body to make ends meet. They became close after several months of working together. She told him she loved him. Many girls say that, but rarely do they mean it. And then came the night of his arrest. She proved just how much she loved him when she spent herself broke paying for his legal defense.

By the time he started serving his sentence, he demanded she get off the streets and marry him. She did exactly as he wished, working a waitressing job at a local Denny's for the entire year he spent locked up. She stuck by him, wrote letters every week and visited the prison every weekend. She was his rock. She paid off the worthless defense attorney's bill from her tips and overtime at the restaurant.

Two years had gone by, and Evita hadn't worked the streets since. Talco was determined she would never again sell her body to pay the rent.

Evita was his angel, a godsend. How could he ever let her go?

Upon his release from prison he made it his mission in life to give her a child. The doctor told them the date of conception for Mateo was probably within the first week of his freedom.

He had never been happier, married to this gorgeous woman whose devotion had withstood every hardship imaginable, and a beautiful son to show for it. If only he could keep it going. If only he could avoid ruining all their lives with his mistakes.

He thought of opening a restaurant; let the New Yorkers have a taste of his wife's fabulous cooking. He'd even name it after her, *Evita's*. With the birth of his son, Mateo Rodriguez, he had new inspiration, a new reason to make something positive of his life. He began plotting and planning.

He spent endless hours working with the Small Business Administration—SBA. They had the business plans, financial plans, and guidance he needed to make it happen. He worked up a menu, designed the graphics for the neon sign, and even calculated twelve month projections of overhead and income. The SBA could provide small loans for business startup, but Talco needed to have a certain amount of his own cash vested in the project. That was the catch. He needed more money.

By his estimates he had two to three months left of running his little *escort service* to save up enough cash to start the restaurant. But that was before the devil sent Oberman and Konowicz into his life to torment him. All his grand plans screeched to a grinding halt when *Los Demonios* began taxing the life out of him, threatening everything he was trying to build.

Evita gave him that angry stare. The girl a real stinger when she knew he was up to something. "Papi, I want you to stop. You don't need the girls. We don't need that much money."

"I know baby, but we're so close. We're almost ready to start the restaurant."

"Papi, how many times do I have to tell you, I don't care about the money. I want us to be happy. If you quit working with the girls you can get rid of those detectives. They can't get to you if you're not doing anything illegal. Don't you see how this is hurting us?"

"Hay corazón, you don't understand how probation works. And these cops are *dirty*. You don't even know how fucked-up they are. It doesn't matter if I'm doing anything illegal. *Los Demonios* can lock me up con nada más que un acusación. I gotta do what they want or I'm goin' back to prison. Ain't no judge or jury for me. If the pigs start pointing fingers, I'll be revoked like that!" He snapped his fingers in demonstration, "That's the way it is."

"Please Papi, just quit it. Do it for me … can't you do it for me?"

"Si, querida. If that's what you want, I'll quit. Right now. I'm done with this shit!" He assured her vehemently. And he meant it. "I'm gonna call all the girls and tell 'em they're on their own. Talco's goin' legit. Next time the detectives call I'll tell 'em to stick it where the sun don't shine!"

* * * *

CHAPTER 13

Konowicz stood with Oberman outside the front door to Bemichis Restaurant with Trish Anstrom, a thirty-something single mom who worked nights as a waitress.

"I saw her pick him up off the ground, and take off running down the street carrying him. It was the damnedest thing ever. Yeah, like I said on the phone, I heard a noise like a gun shot, and by the time I got a chance to look out the door here, that's what I saw. I think the police arrived a few minutes later. I couldn't really see well. It was midnight and the streetlamp is over there." She pointed across the road to the light post, huffed another huge whiff off her cigarette and continued, "Like I mentioned on the phone, I hope it wasn't Aaron. But he hasn't been to work since he left that night, and all this happened not ten minutes after he walked out the door." Finishing her cigarette, she reached into her pack for another one to light from the still glowing butt of the first.

Konowicz addressed her, "So let me see if I got all the facts straight. His name is Aaron Pilan, he's twenty-two years old, about five feet eleven inches, approximately one hundred seventy pounds with dark brown hair and eyes, lives in the Reisner Apartment Building over on 52nd street, about ten blocks down. He doesn't answer calls or text messages, and his voicemail is full. He was last seen leaving here at midnight August 26th, and somebody called asking for him. You think it was his roommate who hasn't seen him in days. Is that correct, Ms. Anstrom?" She nodded yes repeatedly through the haze of cigarette smoke.

"Was there anything you could think of to add to this? Have you ever seen the woman who you said, *picked him up and ran off with him*? Did you recognize her?" Konowicz pressed, still evidencing a slight nasal quality to his speech.

She finished her second cigarette, stomping it out in the planter, and again shook her head no. "Like I said before, I'm not even sure it was Aaron."

Oberman showed Trish the artist's rendering of a blonde woman. "Do you recognize her? Was this the girl you saw that night?"

She frowned. "Maybe. Couldn't see real well. I really can't say for sure."

"Do you have any pictures of Aaron?"

She started shaking her head. "Wait a minute." She turned and entered the restaurant, motioning them to follow.

"Here, on the wall, a picture from a wedding party we did a couple months ago. I'm sure Aaron's in it."

"Yeah, dat's him alright," Oberman mumbled to Konowicz.

Konowicz turned to her abruptly. "Thank you for your time, Ms. Anstrom, you've been very helpful."

"You'll let me know if you find out anything? He's such a sweet boy. I'm worried about him."

"Sure thing. We'll be in touch." Konowicz's toothy smile did not reach his eyes.

* * * *

In the evening, as their official workday came to a close, Konowicz brought glad tidings to his partner, dropping a scrap of paper with a scrawled note on his desk.

"I got the address connected to that cell phone for the Pilan kid. He's in number 204 at the Reisner Apartments. You got time to go pay a visit?" Konowicz smiled at Oberman. He could feel they were getting real close.

Oberman grinned, his first genuine smile of the day. "Looks like we're doin' some overtime."

* * * *

"Hello, I'm Detective Oberman and this is Detective Konowicz. We're with the 124th precinct, New York P.D. We'd like to ask you a few questions if you don't mind. May we come in?"

Kyle instantly went on guard. These two characters looked like they had real badges, but he smelled something malicious and sinister—apart from their body odor. He didn't trust them enough to allow entry.

"Well, I'm not sure what this is all about. Is there a problem?" He didn't like the idea of these two inside the door. They were pushy. Oberman actually slid his foot in the door as they stood there staring down Kyle with their you-don't-want-to-mess-with-us looks. He stared right back and let them continue speaking from the hallway.

"We're here to see Aaron Pilan. Is he here now? We need to talk with him."

That struck him weird. Aaron was about as harmless and law-abiding as they came. He couldn't imagine what these two might possibly want with Aaron. He paused for a moment, and then decided to play along.

"No, actually he's not. Um … I haven't seen him in days. If he's in trouble I'd like to know about it, and how I can help. He's a good friend." His instinctive reaction was to make sure they didn't catch Aaron by surprise.

"You know anything about his involvement with this woman?" Oberman showed Kyle the artist's rendering of Michelle and pushed his bulk into the door a couple more inches. Kyle held his ground, letting the door push up against his body as he tried to look casually at what was a pretty damn accurate drawing of Michelle. He pretended not to notice how they watched him, or how they tried to force their way into his door. They pretended to care about his rights and privacy. None of them were very good actors.

"No, I've never seen her before. Can you tell me what this is all about?" He knew if he gave up Michelle he'd be giving up Aaron, so he continued to stonewall.

"Look, we know he was with her a week ago. We know he lives at this address. We can't go into details because of the on-going investigation. If you know somethin' and you're not telling us, it's only gonna hurt Aaron in the end. If you wanna help your friend, you need to help us find him." Oberman played the standard authoritarian manipulation game.

Kyle knew there was very little these two creeps could do to help Aaron. Cops like this rarely ever helped anyone but themselves.

"I've already told you I don't know anything. I haven't seen him or heard from him in days. His cell phone is disconnected. I don't know what else I can do to help you." He put more pressure on the door, forcing Oberman to back up a couple inches.

Konowicz stepped toward Kyle menacingly, as if he would shove past Oberman and force his way through the door. "Listen here. We're gonna find out everything eventually. We'll find out all about you, your friends, and all the comings and goings here at your little bachelor pad. I'm pretty sure we're gonna find somethin' you won't like. Maybe one of your buddies smokes weed, snorts a little blow, maybe someone's poppin' somebody else's prescription pills. It's a given. You would do a lot more for yourself and your friends if you cooperate with us."

"I don't do drugs, and I don't hang out with losers that do," he informed them calmly. He waved his hand in dismissal of their bullshit. "You can threaten all you want, I don't know where Aaron is and there's nothing illegal happening at my apartment."

Konowicz snapped back, losing his cool, "If I learn you've been lying to us, I'll book your ass for obstruction of justice so fast it'll make your head spin! You'll sit in lock-up just long enough to lose your job and this shit-hole apartment you squat in! Don't fuck with me punk!"

"I've said all I have to say. I'm done with you. Good day, Officers." He shoved the door in the detective's faces. He heard cursing and some back and forth whispering, and then they slipped a note under the door with an N.Y.P.D. business card.

Call me with any new information you get about Aaron Pilan and the woman. Scott Konowicz

Kyle stood there for a moment, debating what to do about the situation. Should he tell them about Michelle? Should he call and leave an anonymous tip? Should he just warn Aaron and stay out of it? The detective's threats seemed to be mostly intimidation tactics. They didn't have anything on him, and he didn't know anything. What you don't know can't hurt you ... right?

Delia overheard parts of the conversation from where she was standing a few feet inside the door. "What was that all about?"

"I'm not sure, but I think Aaron's in trouble and it's got something to do with Michelle."

* * * *

"You have a voicemail from your friend Kyle. He wants you to call as soon as possible. Is very important." Michelle handed Aaron her iPhone after dialing Kyle's number.

"Hey, Kyle, it's Aaron. Got your message. What's goin' on?"

Kyle explained what happened with the two detectives, and then told Aaron how he felt about them and their threats. "Dude, I'm freakin' out! They weren't messin' around! It seems pretty serious. They were talking about *abstraction* of justice! Like they were gonna arrest me! I didn't know anything, so I couldn't tell them anything. Is there something I should know? What's goin' on?"

"I have no idea. Seriously." *Shit, shit, shit!*

"Really? So ... how's it goin' with Michelle?"

Kyle had a suspicious tone to his voice. Aaron wondered what he was thinking. What kind of assumptions he must be making by now.

"Ahhmm ... She's great, we're good. I'm telling you the truth, Kyle. I have no idea what those guys want. Honestly, this is a total surprise. But hey, thanks for blocking for me, I appreciate it. I really owe you one. Maybe I should get an attorney to call and find out what's up." *Shit! What the fuck do I do now? What if they find us?*

Aaron's mind raced through possibilities. He didn't know what to say. He felt like a fugitive in hiding every second that he lied to Kyle. He didn't have a clue what to do if the detectives ever tracked him or Michelle down.

Kyle replied, "Okay, man, cool. Just be careful. I'm telling you those guys are creepy as hell. I had to take a couple shots of Patron to calm down after they left. Oh ... yeah ... um ... Delia's here. She wants to talk to you for a minute."

"Kyle, wait. I gotta go. I don't have time for her right now."

"Hi, Aaron, are you okay? Those officers sounded serious."

He wasn't prepared to deal with Delia. He'd written her off as a thing of the past.

"Uh, yeah, I'm fine. *We're fine.*" He wanted off the phone so he could talk to Michelle. He had a whopping crisis to avert, namely being hunted down by NYPD for assaulting an officer. He hoped that by referring to both him and Michelle as being *fine* together, Delia might catch the subtle hint and leave him alone.

"Hey, Aaron, um ... I was hoping we could meet and talk. I want to talk about ... things between us. Everything has happened so quickly. I've been thinking about you. About us."

"There's not much to say. You broke up with me. You wanted to see other people. It wasn't what I wanted, but now everything's changed. *I've changed.* I thought you wanted your freedom?"

She laughed nervously and stammered, "Well, yeah, but ... I understand that you're angry. I would be too. I want you to know I think I was wrong. I want to see you again. It's hard to talk over the phone ... she's probably there with you right now ... listening. Can we talk in private? Can you come see me tonight? I'm here at the apartment." She sounded like she was starting to beg. It was kinda creepy. She had never been like this before.

Aaron cut her off. "Delia, I'm not mad at you. I was, but it's over now."

"I'm not asking you out on a date, okay. I think we need a chance to talk. It's only been two weeks since we split up. Please Aaron. I really need to see you. I want to make it up to you. It's all my fault. I'll do anything you want ..."

"Listen, this is a really bad time right now. I've gotta get off the phone. There's nothing to talk about. Michelle is really good to me. I've moved on. I'm sorry but I gotta go. I'll call back, maybe, in a couple days or somethin'. Take care. Bye." He hung up on her.

* * * *

Kyle could see the wheels turning in Delia's head. It wasn't difficult to figure out what had happened. If Kyle had a sexy thing like Michelle in his life, he'd drop Delia like a bad habit.

Kyle imagined that devious little mind of hers cooking up a scheme to get her hands on Aaron again. He'd told Aaron more than once she was a selfish brat. It took Michelle's influence to finally pull him from Delia's manipulations and mind games. *What was she up to now? Was she bold enough to do something stupid with those nasty detectives?*

"Hey, Delia, I know how you feel about this. Everything happened so suddenly with Aaron moving out, and you were real close for so long. I hope you're not thinking of doing something with those cops. Don't mess with them, Delia. You call those detectives and you're playing with fire. Besides you could get Aaron in trouble too. Not just Michelle. Let him live his life. If he's making mistakes, let him deal with it. He's not yours to play with anymore. You let him go and now he's gone. You hear what I'm saying? Don't get involved!"

"Alright already! I heard you. You don't have to go into a fit about it. I never said I was gonna do anything! And I can talk to him if I want to. She doesn't own him!"

But Delia wouldn't look him in the eyes.

* * * *

"Is wise that you stay away from the girl. She is dangerous, very selfish. I can see she will be a *problème* if you get involved with her again." Michelle looked Aaron directly in the eyes to see how he reacted to her advice.

"Do I detect a hint of jealousy?" Aaron asked with a smirk.

"You know she's not right for you. Is very difficult to have close relations with people. They are not like us." She pursed her lips in admonishment as though above such petty jealousies. "Is true I care for you. We are bonded. What affects you affects me. But I could never be jealous about this girl. She is an *enfant terrible*, a spoiled child. And she has an obsession with you."

Aaron grinned at her admission. "You are jealous," he chuckled. "Admit it, maybe a little?"

He kissed her on the lips and stroked his fingers through her hair. "You're right, as usual. She is silly, and immature, and there is nothing for you to be jealous about. You know you own my ass. Besides, she could never pull off that stunt you did up against the wall the other night. That was insane. After that performance, how could Delia compare?" The brat enjoyed teasing her. He was gaining confidence in his new life.

"Aaron … do you still have feelings for this girl?"

His nonchalant comment made her sick to her stomach. "I hate the thought I take away your choices." Her voice fell to a whisper. "I do not wish to 'own your ass' as you say so crudely."

"Aww, Michelle, ma belle." He smiled as he ran his fingers over her jawline. "No, no, no. Really, I don't think of Delia for even a minute. You're the only one who gets my attention. You're the one I want. Is that what you want to hear?"

"Mmm … *Oui*." She smiled as he played with her.

"So what about the real issue? The police." Aaron gave her the raised eyebrow.

"They are just as silly and stupid as the girl, but very dangerous. If they become a *problème*, we will deal with them or move on. I am not a murderer, but I have no *problème* with taking out the trash."

* * * *

Detective Grayson walked up to Konowicz's desk and slapped down a sticky note, "Got a message for you. It came in while you were on the other line. Says, *The girl you are looking for with blond hair and green eyes works with EZ Escort services and her name is Michelle.* I got the phone number to EZ from her too, but she didn't say her name. Wanted to remain anonymous." One look at Konowicz and he chuckled.

"Oh shit! Is that the prize fighter who knocked you on your ass the other day? Ha! That's fuckin' priceless. When you catch up with her tell her I said thanks!" Grayson slapped Konowicz on the shoulder laughing at him. Konowicz's busted nose throbbed from the jolt.

* * * *

CHAPTER 14

"My, my, my, *très* sexy. Don't you look nice! I like this shirt on you. The blue is your best color." Michelle turned Aaron in a circle as she checked him out for his big date.

"Yeah, I do look pretty damn good, don't I? I'm dead sexy." He spanked his ass in the mirror as Michelle grinned. His new eight hundred dollar outfit made a distinct impression. He had never realized how much clothes can make the man. Michelle had a sharp eye for fashion, and a deep pocketbook.

"Thank you so much, I never could've bought this on my dime." He smiled as she ran her hands over the ass of his black slacks.

Michelle never seemed to care about money. She was constantly shopping for expensive designer clothes for the both of them. She paid all the taxi rides, and who knew how much her apartment cost. He never bothered to ask about money. He didn't have the first clue about her finances beyond the fact that she made good money on her dates.

He stared at her sideways in the mirror as she smiled back. *Who is this woman that I'm in love with?* He didn't even know how old she truly was, or so much as her full name. The woman was a mystery, but that's the way she liked it.

Michelle broke him out of his silent reverie with her speech on vampire etiquette. "*Mon petit chou.* Remember the rules. Feed no more than sixty seconds. No multiple orgasms—you risk the addiction. Release her when she *pops.* Not a moment longer. Avoid sex. Is a very bad idea. Your control is not good right now. Trust me when I tell you, is bad. You don't want to hurt a woman that way."

"Yes, Massa. Aye's a good slave, Massa. Don't beat me!" He pinched her ass as he teased.

"I want you to save your energy for later tonight. I have something planned. Some more tricks for you. We will need your stamina!"

He envisioned the many things she had taught him in the bedroom. Wild passionate sex for hours and hours on end. He shivered in anticipation, adjusting his pants as he caught a semi just thinking about her.

* * * *

"Nice to meet you, Mrs. Callahan. My name is Aaron. How are you this evening?" He met his *date* in the lounge of the Double Tree Inn. The music hadn't begun yet and the quiet unpopulated ambience felt peaceful, romantic.

She hugged him, planting a kiss on his cheek—a little too familiar to be completely cordial. She replied with an inviting expression. "Fantastic now you're here, honey. Aren't you the sexiest thing I've seen in years? Look at you!" She held his hand as she stepped back in appreciation of his physical assets.

Reading her mind, he found her fascinating. His first official *date* as an escort. He dug in deep, trying to get a sense of her entire being in addition to her current thoughts, which were mostly occupied with fantasies of sex with him. He clearly read several key components of her soul. She'd been married for twenty years to a jet-set corporate CEO. The asshole preferred sex with his secretaries and assistants to her. Of course, it hadn't always been that way. Her husband had developed the habit over the years, gradually growing distant. She'd thought of divorcing him many times over, but their kids kept her from going through with it. This wonderful forty-plus mother of three lived daily with emotional and sexual neglect, much the same as him. Well, up until a week ago.

He sympathized with her instantly. He couldn't fault her for hiring an escort. And why exactly was she interested in him? Discretion. She could afford expensive eye candy that guaranteed discretion and allowed her to enjoy life's simple pleasures of sexual fulfillment with a hard body half her age. It wasn't love, but it would have to do.

He realized immediately he would break his promise to Michelle. He couldn't refuse this woman the very thing she needed most, Michelle's warnings be damned. He vowed to maintain control and give her what she was *paying* for.

She planned to spend the evening at the hotel. Dinner, cocktails, dancing, and then retire up to the room. At five hundred an hour, she intended to pay cash for four hours. The escort service had already charged their fee in advance. His cash would be his to keep.

The dinner went smoothly with small talk about her family and business interests. She drifted into politics that flew completely over his head. He mostly just listened to her. She was a truly remarkable woman and he had grown to genuinely like her.

They danced for a time, slow and intimate, stealing kisses here and there. Her hands began to roam below his waistline. "Why don't we head up to the room?"

"You must be reading my mind." She had such a beautiful smile to complement her aching soul. He wondered what kind of asshole would treat a woman like this so poorly.

This woman needed him. She needed him to make this a special night for her. She seemed so wonderful, only wishing to be loved. He was willing to test his tenuous control, for her.

Upstairs, she kissed him on the lips. "Call me Rosalie, Mrs. Callahan is so formal, makes me feel like I'm talking to one of my son's friend's. I'm going to get changed into something more comfortable. I'll be back in a moment."

She exited the bathroom a few moments later wearing a red see-through negligee with a matching sheer G-string. Rosalie wasted no time. She kissed him deeply while her hands undressed him fast and efficient. She had a definite plan for the night's activities and followed it without hesitation or embarrassment.

Rosalie looked him up and down with another one of her beautiful smiles blooming across her face as he stood before her naked. He enjoyed seeing himself from her perspective as she ogled his body. She loved his trim abs that didn't fold over his belt like Mr. Callahan's. And his firm pecs, they didn't need one of those compression t-shirts to hide man-boobs. When her attention settled on his cock she licked her lips. The woman couldn't wait to get him in her mouth. He was the best date she'd ever had through the agency.

If he could perform like the stud she imagined, she'd definitely be coming back for another date. After a few seconds of appreciation and wild imaginings, she put her skillful hands to work caressing him, bringing him to full size.

As she pushed him back onto the bed, she climbed over him and said, "I love fellatio; it's a specialty of mine. I can't resist wrapping my lips around something so beautiful." With that she went down on him. She took the top position working him voraciously. He lay back and let her do as she pleased. She toyed with him, licking up and down his length, teasing, and then concentrating intense suction on the very tip. He moaned and couldn't help but fist his hand in her hair and lift his hips as she tugged on the head of his cock. She pulled away, teeth, tongue and lips scraping past his most sensitive flesh to come up for air with a smile on her face.

"Honey, I can do this all night long."

Then she went right back at it, a muffled, vibrating groan massaging him as she went all the way down, craning her neck to accommodate his full length.

He read her desire to receive the same treatment she gave him. Never leaving her mouth, he pivoted into position, his face buried between her legs as Michelle taught him. He took his time. His fingers toyed with her entry and stroked her inner thighs. Pulling her panties aside, he bared her flesh to his taste.

Rosalie worked his whole length frantically, sliding up and down, in and out, faster and faster. He entered her with his fingers while suckling and nibbling at her folds. Their intensity reached fever pitch when she peaked, screaming her release into his erection, clamping down on him forcefully. The vibrations and fierceness of her reaction brought him fast. He poured himself deep into her throat, his hand trapping the back of her head tightly. She wanted to be crammed down on his cock. She wanted to swallow it. It was something her husband had done so often that she had grown to crave this form of submission. Rosalie really did enjoy fellatio. She suspected it was the primary reason her husband married her.

After a moment's reprieve, both of them catching their breath, he shifted position to roll them over while Rosalie worked him by hand back to full readiness. He fought with control. He wanted so badly to pin her down and screw her until she begged him to stop. He wanted to bite her over and over and over. Michelle wasn't kidding. Managing sex and feeding together might prove impossible. His need reared its ugly head, like another personality taking over, a predator that wanted to use and abuse poor little Rosalie Callahan, heedless of her frailty. He began to regret his decision. He feared what harm he might do to this wonderful woman.

Then she slipped a condom on him and opened her legs wide in invitation. All control slipped. The beast took over, pure need, desire, lust and hunger. An undeniable driving hunger that wiped away all reason.

He slid into Rosalie fast and hard, sinking in all the way to her limit in one swift thrust. He kept on going, a wicked tight grip on her luscious hips. He pounded her flesh as she screamed and writhed in the throes of the wildest sex she'd ever known. He abused her silken flesh with the abandon of super-human strength. As he thrust into her, burying himself all the way with his climax, he remembered his foolish ideas of control. Rosalie screamed at the top of her lungs as he chomped down on her neck and drank deeply, consuming her blood, ecstasy, and passion in a magical blend.

When he regained a little sanity, he assessed the damage. Rosalie lay below him quivering and writhing. Her breath came in hoarse pants, an animal sound. Searching through her mind, he was relieved to find he hadn't hurt her.

Rosalie had experienced cataclysmic sex, but she didn't seem to be any worse for it. Maybe sore, in a good way, but no lasting hurt, and most importantly, she hadn't acquired the addiction, not like Lisa. Ignoring the fact that he'd barely restrained himself from killing her, he judged his experiment a success.

He dressed after cleaning himself up in the restroom and returned to check on Rosalie. She was still breathing heavily, but had regained some semblance of normalcy. Her body continued to vibrate and twitch with sensory overload and her eyes were dilated and glazed, drunk with pleasure. He watched her for a few moments as she caught her breath.

"OH ... MY ... GOD! I'm ... I ... I don't know how you did it, but that's the most amazing sex I've ever had. Whatever you got, honey, they should be bottling and selling it for billions. I'd get up to see you on your way, but I'm not moving from this bed tonight. I wouldn't be able to stand up even if there was a fire."

He felt damn proud of himself right at that moment.

"I'm pleased to be at your service. I had hoped to give you a special evening. You're a good woman. You deserve a few special moments in your life. Whoever is neglecting you isn't worthy of your time and attention."

"I've known that for years, honey, but we can't always get what we want. Tonight you've done that for me. You've given me more than I ever expected and it was just what I needed. Would you hand me my purse, please." She pulled out three thousand dollars in fifties and handed it to him as he kissed her goodbye.

He noticed how much money she was shoving at him. "This is way too much!" She had already provided both her body and her precious life's blood. Taking her money felt wrong.

"Baby, what you got is priceless. I would gladly pay more. You're worth every penny and then some." She smiled at him sweetly. A woman with a smile like that deserved so much more from life. "I hope to see you again. Would that be possible in a couple weeks?" In her mind she debated whether or not she could handle another session with him and not suffer a stroke or heart attack. The boy had fucked her senseless.

"Yes, I would like that very much. You know how to make the arrangements. Until then, take care, and get some rest." He blew her a kiss and walked out the door.

He knew he needed his strength for what Michelle had planned, so he fed twice more on the dance floor on his way out of the hotel. Aaron's spirits soared. He rode a high of blood and sex as he hailed a taxi cab for the ride home to Michelle.

* * * *

CHAPTER 15

In the taxi on the way home, Aaron contemplated the wonder of his new life. To live without need for the trappings of civilization, food, and drink. To be free of the disease of greed driving every moment and motivation. To have power over all you encounter, both physical superiority and the power to live without want. The only need that could not be ignored was that of the blood, easily remedied in an instant.

Money, houses, cars, consumerism, what need did he have for any of these things? People gave him anything he asked for. Anything he needed or desired was his for the taking. What did he really need? Shelter, clothing, blood, nothing more and nothing he could not take or borrow at any moment. What did he desire? Blood and the sensual contact that naturally followed. It was his right, his due, and it could not be withheld.

Was existence free of hardship and privation any way to live? Where was the need for things and money that had once propelled him out the door to work every day? The need for approval and love driving him to chase Delia so fruitlessly? What was life without need? Could it be said that he really lived at all without the burden of these afflictions? These discomforts experienced by the less fortunate?

In truth, his existence wasn't entirely carefree. His autonomy ended where Michelle's began. Being her slave, her servant, was the great misfortune that defined his life, giving distinct flavor to all his moments of freedom and triumph. Yet he wasn't bitter. He loved her for all that she was, mistakes and attitudes included. All things considered, being Michelle's slave was the most fulfilling and enjoyable life he'd ever known.

Aaron entered the apartment bouncing with anticipation, his mind filled with fantasies of what Michelle might have in store for him. He felt comfortable and secure knowing this was his home and he shared it with a magnificent woman whom he loved deeply.

Michelle didn't carry the same pleasant *home-coming* mindset. Something was very wrong. Her mind had closed off and he read only an icy-cold, blank wall from her. It was the first time in days she had closed down like this.

"You look very happy tonight. Very satisfied. I hope you didn't ruin your appetite. I have something special for you, my special boy." Michelle patted him on the cheek with a gleam in her eye and a tightlipped grin.

He grinned back at her sheepishly, thinking of the energy he'd expended during those gratuitous moments with Rosalie. He thought he was spry enough to handle whatever she had in store for him. His appetite for Michelle held strong as ever. Michelle watched him closely. He thought he saw something in her eyes, a burning ember sparking into flame.

She turned and marched into the bedroom speaking over her shoulder, "Come take off your clothes. Sunrise in two hours!" This was not a request. It was an order.

They came to bed nude, sliding under the covers side by side. A remote coldness permeated Michelle's every move. Even her skin seemed cooler to the touch. Their connection was devoid of any warmth or mutual affection. His hackles rose. What should have been sensual and arousing now seemed menacing. She gave him a feeling of wariness, as though she'd pounce at any moment.

"Is there something wrong? Are you angry with me?"

She slid her hands over his chest and reached down between his legs to feel him. Her hand came up. She ran her fingers under her nose, catching the scent.

"What have you done to anger me?" Michelle had a strange look on her face.

"Well ... I did have a little bit of fun with my date ..."

He braced himself for the onslaught, expecting her to tear into him with a scathing lecture. Instead she asked calmly, "Just a little fun?"

He nodded his head, thoroughly confused. Michelle flashed her eyes, a brief glimpse of animosity bleeding through her privacy wall, but she quickly clamped down her iron control.

In a cold, quiet voice barely above a whisper, she asked-compelled, "Did you hurt the woman?"

He tried to issue a straightforward denial, but what came out of his mouth was, "Maybe a little bit ..."

As soon as he spoke, two vivid images flashed to his mind's eye, transmitted directly to Michelle. The first was of his hard cock in his hand as he stood in the shower cleaning up after his date. A pinkish-red taint of blood rinsed down the drain from his groin. He had made Rosalie bleed from her womb. The second image was of Rosalie lying on her back quivering and moaning, distinct hand-grip marks visible on both her thighs. He hadn't really been cognizant of the damage he did to Rosalie until Michelle forcibly extracted the truth from the recesses of his mind.

Michelle had that gleam, a wild look, like she was about to take a chunk out of his hide. She didn't. She reached between his legs to grab ahold of his cock.

"I will be on top this time, lie back and enjoy the ride!" She spoke in a virtual hiss.

His instincts screamed of impending danger, stripping him of any arousal. He was completely flaccid.

"Give me your full erection now!" Michelle growled as though ordering soldiers to stand at attention. This was a first. He knew a threshold had been crossed. She had never used her authority to impose her will in their intimacy. Michelle was rewriting the boundaries of their relationship and he was sure to be on the losing side of the fence. Upon her spoken command, his penis reacted of its own accord, growing to full tilt readiness without any sexual arousal whatsoever. Fear, shame, and a desire to run created a sickening boil in his gut.

This must be what it feels like to be raped.

Michelle gradually worked him, first licking and sucking slowly, sensually. Then she sped up her ministrations until the intensity reached super-human speed and force. She shifted position, straddling his face with her thighs to place her most intimate flesh in his face, and began grinding herself back and forth across his lips and teeth. His natural reaction of arousal spiraled up. The wonderful sensations of Michelle's highly skilled attentions could not be denied. All his fears erased in the heat of the moment.

At the point he reached his peak and could no longer resist his climax, Michelle struck like a viper, driving her mouth down to seal against the base of his engorged sex to the ultimate deep throat position. With this move she buried her razor sharp fangs deep into his pubic flesh, sinking in *to the bone,* sucking down his blood and climax all together.

Aaron's peak, pain, shock, and venom-saturated loins, brought the most excruciatingly intense orgasm he'd ever known. Without conscious thought, his vampiric instincts reacted. He sunk his fangs into Michelle's intimate folds, digging down through inner and outer labia to hit home at her pelvic bone. He gave as good as he got, blasting Michelle with the same intensity of climax twisted by pain, shock and the amplified sexual effects of his venom flooding through her tender, vaginal flesh.

Both Aaron and Michelle's psychic barriers of privacy shattered in the storm of sensations and pain. Mind-altering waves of ecstasy, agony, and multiple orgasms assaulted them. Each experienced the other's rollercoaster of peaks simultaneously with their own. The cycle of climax, crash, and repeated climax continued over and over again. The lovers remained locked together, spasming and grinding, consuming each other's blood and sex until their physical limits of endurance were reached and surpassed. Sometime near sunrise they passed into oblivion, still locked in each other's parasitic embrace.

Both awoke at sunset, faces buried in each other's groins. Michelle arose first and silently prepared a scorching hot bath. They looked like hell—their faces and thighs encrusted in blood and sex, their expressions identically haunted, somber. Aaron sat in the oversized Jacuzzi across from Michelle. They soaked in silence, avoiding eye contact. He didn't know what had happened. His world traversed from one extreme of happiness to the other extreme of pain, humiliation, and depravity.

When he finished bathing and moved to leave the tub, Michelle broke the silence. "What did you do to that woman last night? I know you had sex with her and I know you hurt her." Her face had twisted in a murderous snarl. Her mind was blocked up solid.

He answered her simply, "Yes … I had sex with Rosalie."

Michelle reached out lightning fast with a whip-snap move to grab hold of his scrotum, her claws piercing through flesh, drawing blood in demonstration of her severity.

"Show me your memories of what you did to her!"

The door to his mental vault dissolved. Their connection opened wide to access his memories, or anything else she might want to know. His mind instantly replayed the entire date with Rosalie leading up to his return home, and then followed by the bizarre sexual encounter with Michelle, transmitting all of it to her via their psychic bond. Michelle experienced all his thoughts, feelings, emotions, and sensations as though she lived through these moments inside his body along with him.

"Enough! I don't need to see anymore!" She turned away from him as if trying to avert her eyes from what she'd witnessed. She released her painful grip on his genitals and his blood turned the bath water pink. Her face looked stricken.

He leaned towards her and whispered, "You're fuckin' nuts."

He climbed out of the bath and dressed without once looking or speaking to Michelle. He ignored the tears of blood silently running down her face.

She had stripped him of all protections, absolute zero privacy. To him it felt like standing naked out in Times Square, all his dirty little secrets laid bare. Psychic rape.

It was the most demeaning thing she could've done, apart from ordering him to kill himself. He settled into heavy depression. He meant nothing to Michelle. Nothing more than a possession—a servant to be punished when he misbehaved.

Shattered, smashed, damaged beyond recognition—Michelle demolished all hope that her affections were genuine. He was nothing but her slave, her property, who had disobeyed and needed to be reprimanded. He felt like a dog pissing on the floor, forced to have his nose rubbed in it to learn a lesson.

"Come, we must feed." Michelle spoke in terse tones. She wouldn't look him in the eyes. Her face was tight-lipped and severe as he followed her out the door.

"Yes, Master." He wasn't teasing or smiling.

Cruising through the night streets in the taxi, his depression began to take on a new color of resentment. Why should he be treated like this? Was this all because he disobeyed her directive or was there something else? Is this how it would be with her for years to come? Being punished for virtually nothing? He deeply resented her abuse of power.

He began to hate Michelle for turning an act of affectionate lovemaking into a sadistic punishment. The kindness and mutual care that once permeated their relationship disappeared. Michelle reached out to hold his hand as she had so many times before, but the gesture no longer felt like the loving caress he'd imagined it to be. It felt like a leash.

* * * *

CHAPTER 16

He arose without a word to Michelle. He had slept on the floor in silent protest. She remained in bed. She didn't say a word when he left, exiting via the fire escape.

He had to get out. Just go, walk, somewhere, anywhere away from her. Every second of every minute, every waking moment she was there. In his thoughts, in his face, the smell of her saturated every corner of the apartment. He couldn't get rid of her scent. It was on his clothes, on his skin, in his blood. *You are blood of my blood.* She owned him. He was marked. He couldn't go anywhere or do anything without her *being there, holding his fucking hand.*

He marched down the alley way, hoping to burn off some steam, put a little distance between them. His temper flared to the point that he burned to lash out in violence. Every word and gesture from her the night before seemed to have a double meaning mocking him and his subservience to her.

This need for violence and confrontation was something wholly new to him. He'd never before felt such fury and frustration. It was a raging passionate fire threatening to overtake all reason. He had to get some distance and cool off before he ended up going after Michelle. He had no illusions about how that would turn out. She'd kill him.

He began jogging down the alley moving through the back streets. He stayed to the dark recesses of the city, purposely avoiding *people*. Oblivious, he passed into one of the seedier areas of New York. This was a place he would never normally walk, especially not in the darkness of night. The new and improved Aaron was unconcerned. He felt absolutely no fear of anyone—apart from Michelle. She'd been telling the truth when she spoke in her condescending tone, *they are like cattle.*

He tried to stop dwelling on the negative, but his mind continued to find things to make him angry, worsening his mood. His problem stemmed from one inescapable source: Michelle. No matter how far he walked she was still there at the edge of his mind, connected, waiting, judging him unjustly.

After some introspection he recognized what the true problem was. Her power over him governed not only his physical body, but his soul as well. No matter that she treated him like a dog to be punished, he still loved her. His heart wouldn't listen to reason. He needed to be near her like he needed air to breathe.

Deep in his soul search, meandering aimlessly through the night, he landed himself in the middle of a group of thugs. They were big, black, tattooed, and not the least bit happy to see him in their neighborhood. A quick scan of their minds revealed they were looking forward to some entertainment at his expense.

By the time he came to his senses, he was surrounded by five black gang members who looked like they spent more time in jail than out. Their pants hung low at the waist, boxer shorts exposed in the classic 'sag' of the urban gangster. He could read their immediate interest in him. They assumed he was easy prey with cash, credit cards, or something else of value.

The one on his right in a NY Jets hat yelled loudly to his companions, "Dis mousy ass bitch must be lost." He turned to Aaron up in his face, pointing at him. "Hey powder, don't you know where da fuck you at?"

The inner city ghetto, one of those places he'd artfully avoided all his life. *Shit.* There were heaps of trash on the ground, buildings with broken and boarded up windows, and isolated pockets of gangsters hanging out in the shadowy corners. Liquor stores lined either side of the street. Not a white person in sight. *The Projects.*

"Fuck!" Aaron cursed under his breath as they closed in around him, cutting off all paths to escape.

The guy directly in front of him wore a black hoodie and was the biggest of the lot, three hundred fifty pounds of muscle and bad attitude. He stepped towards Aaron with a wicked scowl that left no doubt of his intentions. The gorilla growled down on him from his six foot six height, "What you got in your pockets, bitch?" Aaron suspected the guy had never been denied such a request before. He had the air of one who always took what he wanted, when he wanted, from whoever he wanted.

Aaron stepped back. "Hey, I don't want any problems."

The guy to the left in a NY Giants coat grabbed Aaron by his arm. "You are the problem."

Aaron reacted instinctively, snapping his arm out to break the hold. He connected hard against the man's chest, a crack-crunch sound. The man's entire body flew backwards several feet, and he landed on his butt, wheezing in pain. The excessive force of Aaron's whip-like reaction surprised him as much as it did the guy he hit.

"Git dat mothafucka!" yelled the guy with French-braided hair. Aaron's aggressive response triggered a free-for-all.

The call to attack punched an adrenaline surge through Aaron. A wildly exhilarating sense of power filled him, a limitless strength and energy. He easily evaded several blows, his movements much faster than theirs by magnitudes. He now understood what Michelle meant when she had stated so eloquently, *they will be turtles, moving in slow motion.*

As they closed in on him, he had no space left to dodge their strikes, and two of them grabbed at his arms. His frustration mounted as he was struck in the head from behind. His desire to lash out and smash these frail meatsacks caught hold, and he roared in rage whipping in a full circle. He momentarily broke their holds which pulled two of them completely off balance. They flew through the air, then scraped and tumbled across the ground.

Cool. He took a moment to watch their bodies roll to a complete stop.

He instinctively sensed the others coming back at him from all directions. He spun again and lashed out with his fists in wild haymaker swings, connecting with three of them in a split second. His blows seemed to have an exaggerated effect. Each thug was sent tumbling away, one flipping end over end through the air. They were rag dolls, and he tossed them around with no real effort.

The two remaining thugs who had escaped his spin move came in from the front and right simultaneously. The man to his right reached him first. With an open handed shove, Aaron sent him flying back through the air. The man landed sprawled on his back, his skull cracked on the asphalt beneath him. *He isn't getting up any time soon.*

Aaron stared in fascination at the powerful effect of a simple one-handed push. As he gawked, the man in front of him dropped low and hit Aaron squarely in a wrestler's tackle. His attention snapped into focus. He instinctively twisted with his legs splayed out wide for balance. Then he flung the attacker out to his side with an instantaneous pivot and shoved hard with both hands.

His maneuver spun them around completely, his attacker's momentum flowing past and out the other direction. The thug went flying through the air to land on the pavement face first with a crunchy thud. Aaron stood solidly on his feet, facing the opposite direction. The graceful redirect had turned him around a hundred eighty degrees.

All five men were down on the pavement hurting. He instinctively wanted to fight to the death, to crush and slice their feeble bodies to pieces as he drank them dry. He tasted the scents of their blood, fear, and adrenaline. They smelled like food.

He shook his head in attempt to break the powerful bloodlust desire surging through his body. His fangs extended fully, mouth wet with venom, ready to feast upon their flesh. He could kill them right now. Drain them of liters of blood in mere seconds. He'd be gone before one of the punk-ass thugs at the liquor store across the street could finish calling 911. It was *so* tempting. And it would be *so* easy. No one would ever know it was him. No one could identify him in this dark setting. The bystanders were too far away to see anything but a white guy dressed in jeans and dark shirt. They couldn't even see his face. The perfect moment for a couple quick kills.

He fought with himself, an internal battle of wills against an urge so powerful he could barely contain it. He growled and snarled, looking back and forth at these slug-like, slow moving *cattle*, struggling with the compulsion to rend and tear flesh. He finally made the snap decision. He redirected his energy into flight, racing back down the alley he had emerged from earlier. In his hurry to escape before he killed someone, he knocked down the man in his path who'd just regained his feet. As he bowled the man over, he heard the crackle-snap of bones breaking. The thug was nothing more than limp flesh against Aaron's charging force. Five of them had been no match for him. The outcome was determined before the confrontation ever began.

He sped down the streets, heading in the direction of home. His powerful bloodlust burned, calling him to smash, tear and rend flesh. He began seeking out new prey. Several heartbeats thumped nearby, ripe for tapping. He sensed all that wonderful juicy goodness just begging to be slurped down. Reason reasserted in his mind, and he realized what he was doing as he snuck up on a man and woman crouched in the alley with their smoking crack pipe. He barely stopped himself at the last moment, running off down the alley in the other direction.

Though he wanted to go home, get off the streets for a few minutes, away from the *food* stench of people, he couldn't return to Michelle with all this tension singing through his body. He stopped in the alley two blocks from home seeking a target for his aggression. The only thing available that wouldn't result in death and mutilation was a steel dumpster sitting against the concrete wall of the alley.

He glanced around to verify there were no witnesses. Having finally found an outlet for his aggression, he funneled it all into that ugly, squatting steel dumpster. He hit it full bore, holding nothing back. He smashed it over and over with his fists, screaming in rage, frustration, and unfulfilled hunger. Each strike left behind a crumpled mess of indentations. As he collapsed the front side of the dumpster, he moved to the left, smashing inward with a barrage of hook punches on each side of the ninety degree corner until it was so misshapen it no longer resembled a rectangle. The lid popped up at a twisted angle, never again to fit down on the mangled receptacle. The front and side of the poor thing had caved inward like a crushed beer can. The irreparable condition of the dumpster testified to the intensity of his frustration. The green-painted steel had absorbed Aaron's crushing force far better than those unfortunate gang members.

Knuckles abraded and raw, sliced open, he watched the damage knit back together right before his eyes. He stared in creeped-out fascination as his knuckles healed up to little pink welts in a matter of minutes. A few minutes and the flesh had completely rejoined over the cuts, leaving only a slight raw spot as evidence of his tantrum. The miracle of vampiric regeneration captured his attention long enough to calm him down. He regained some badly needed serenity. Finally, he could go home and spend another night beneath the yoke of his master.

The dumpster workout session had mostly satisfied his desire to lash out at something. He no longer felt the overwhelming need for violence. The incident proved a nice little distraction. His new concern was that Michelle might learn of his misadventures in the street, causing another point of contention between them. He focused on slowing down his breathing and closed his mind securely within the vault prior to entering the apartment.

He knew she sensed his tension, but wasn't aware of the new source for it. She attempted to make an opening. "Are you ready to talk about this *problème?*"

He clammed up, not wanting to betray his actions to her inadvertently, but a sliver of irritation slipped through the vault door. *Bullshit, she knew exactly what was wrong ... her.* Despite this spike of emotion he answered coldly, "I'm fine. Eerything is fine ... Are we going to feed soon?"

He was hungry for blood. The sooner they fed the better.

He monitored her thoughts closely as Michelle considered pressuring him to draw out the unspoken issues between them. He read her concern, she worried he was a little too edgy, volatile. She let it go, for now. "*Oui*, another night club. You need more practice with *control*. Get dressed. I will be ready soon."

He didn't respond. He changed quickly and stood at the door waiting unobtrusively. Beyond the need to feed, he had no excitement or anticipation for their outing. Another evening of nightlife, tethered to his master.

* * * *

CHAPTER 17

Michelle watched Aaron as he kept his distance from her, cold and sterile, going along to get along. After three nights like this, she reached the limit of her patience for his brooding silence. She had attempted to engage him in conversation but he blocked her, refusing to speak unless asked a direct question. His mind remained closed off, not a hint of his thoughts. Only the slightest taint slipped past his barrier once in a while. These small glimpses of his thoughts never contained anything positive.

He was going sour fast.

Something needed to change soon before they reached an impasse where she might be forced to take action. She might have to kill him.

She learned more from his aura than from their psychic bond. It was streaked with bold colors of anger and resentment. She'd never seen this side of him before. His cold negativity saturated everything. Their time together had become mechanical, holding no elements of friendliness. They went through the motions of meeting their basic feeding impulse then returned to Michelle's apartment in silence.

Michelle briefly considered ending it now. She'd done it before. It wasn't impossible to kill a vampire. Maybe difficult, but not impossible. With her authority of compulsion she held the advantage despite his superior strength and speed. It would be quick, painless. He wouldn't suffer. Perhaps that was the humane thing to do. He obviously wasn't happy living under her domination. He looked like he was ready to take her head off at any moment. Maybe it was wise to strike first before he turned on her.

He sat at the kitchen table in front of her laptop, his attention absorbed by the Internet. She flexed her razor sharp claws and reached for him. He had his back turned, his beautiful shirtless torso exposed to her attack. She could do it so quick he'd never see it coming. She envisioned the move in her mind's eye, marshaling her nerve to do it. Then he sensed her there right behind him, his breathing quickened, his heart rate elevated. His aura bled through with colors of anxiety, angst, frustration, lust, and there it was, faint but still recognizable, love. He was fighting with the fact that he still loved her despite everything she'd done to him. His internal battle slipped past the crack in his mental vault. It confirmed what she saw in his aura. He loved her, and resented the fact.

And he was hurting.

It occurred to her that she had become the cruel master, abusing her power over him. She remembered being in the same position, enslaved by a sadist. And what was the difference? She had turned sex into a torturous form of punishment. What made her any better than her former master?

She realized she was the one to blame for the situation between them. She would need to make the effort to repair the breach. It was her responsibility. She owed him an apology.

But what if he remained cold and aloof? Had she created a monster? Was it too late already? What if she'd led him too far down the path of cruelty?

She wanted the old Aaron back. The one who looked at her with such adoration, not the cold resentful bastard he'd become. She enjoyed him in her life. They were good together. The few nights they had spent in her bed were fantastic. The most invigorating moments of the past five decades. She decided to take the initiative to break through to him.

"We need to talk about what happened the other night." She stepped around to face him and looked directly into his eyes. "Things cannot remain as they are between us."

He didn't answer. He continued giving her the silent treatment. His emotions boiled behind the door to his mental vault.

* * * *

Aaron felt like a dumb animal who still loves its master regardless of whatever abuse it must endure. No matter how angry he was, he still loved Michelle. This made him even angrier. He felt like tearing something apart with his bare hands in frustration. The sad truth: he ached to be near her. But what good would it do to behave like an affectionate sop when dealing with a mercenary who uses sex as punishment? And so he bottled it up. Anger, resentment, love, lust, desire, it was becoming quite a toxic blend.

Part of his problem was the extreme sexual frustration of being so close to her without intimacy. He'd slept on the floor of her bedroom for two days in a row. If it were possible he would have slept on the couch, but her bedroom was the only room sealed against the daylight. Lying near her, knowing she was there but so distant, had become an especially agonizing form of torture. He wanted to hurt her, love her, fuck her every which way and leave her, all at the same time.

Instead he did nothing and said nothing. He didn't have a clue how to talk to her without blowing up in her face.

"I fear I have made a mess, and I must explain." She paused considering her words carefully. "My only experience with the male vampire was very disturbing. He was my master, extremely violent, with no control over his passions. The night he turned me, he did horrible things to me. When my body was completely broken and I bled almost to death, only then did he feed me his blood. I soon learned this was normal for him. He abused the frail women all the time. He said this is the vampire's way because our passions consume all reason. He claimed is worse with the males. They are always mixing sex, blood, and violence. It was a very long time before I realized he was simply justifying his monstrous behavior."

Aaron felt disgusted and compassionate with her confession. He wanted to reach out to her, but did not. The hurt and resentment hung between them like a wall.

He broke his silence. "You believed I would behave this way with Rosalie? Yes, I suppose you did, considering what happened with Lisa." He still felt ashamed about what he'd done to the dancer. His guilt weighed upon him. And then there was Rosalie, who he'd also hurt inadvertently. He began to see the danger he posed to women, how Michelle might view his indiscretions. He knew with certainty he could have killed Lisa or Rosalie, and he might have even enjoyed it.

"Lisa was nothing compared to what I have seen, what I experienced through my master." She reached out to him, caressing his face and hair, trying to impart some affection. "I assumed you did something terrible to Rosalie. I never imagined you could have the caution and compassion you showed her. I felt your thoughts and experiences with her. You tried very hard for control." She stepped closer to him, looking him in the eyes while she continued touching him. He finally stood up and faced her.

"What you did was beautiful. In a way she loves you for this gift you give her. I must apologize to you."

She hadn't come to shove it in his face like he'd expected. She was asking forgiveness. The dam of emotion started to break, resentment, anger, and hopelessness leaking out. "What difference does it make? You can force me to do whatever you want, whenever you feel like it. Why does it matter what I think?"

"It matters to me." She opened her own mental privacy block to let him feel the truth of her words. Her sincerity seemed at odds with her behavior of the last two days, he struggled to believe it.

His rancor overflowed, pouring all over her. He laughed bitterly. "I shouldn't really complain, the sex was awesome. A bit painful, but still phenomenal."

He stuck her with his nasty, sarcastic barb, but she let it slide, reaching past the negativity, trying to find the other side of his emotions. Michelle stepped up to full body contact nuzzling his neck. She was cheating again, using the power of his attraction for her to wash away all the spite and resentment.

She whispered in his ear brushing her lips across his skin. "Yes, it was wonderful. Yet I hurt you. I fear I have done something you will never forgive. I was wrong. My only excuse is that I was very angry. I assumed you abused Rosalie. I wanted to punish you, to abuse you. And I did."

Her body language unraveled three days of loneliness and frustration. The physical power she held over him with her touch was so complete she didn't even need to speak, but she continued with her apology anyway.

"I understand how you feel, but I must beg your forgiveness. I promised I would not abuse you, and I broke my promise." Michelle began kissing his neck and stroking his back and shoulders and chest.

She cheated hardcore. Impossible to remain angry when she poured on the affection. All his resentment and pain drained away at the touch of her warm wet lips and fingertips. Second by second, he lost each and every reason he held for being angry. All that remained was love and forgiveness. He could never deny her forgiveness. He couldn't think of much else when she did this to him. He had no defense for her secret weapon. Her seduction was irresistible.

"You promise you're not gonna do that again? You promise you won't judge me based on assumption? You promise not to abuse your power?" He tried to hold her at arm's length to give her a serious look.

She snaked back into his arms, whispering in his ear, flicking her tongue. "I promise. I am forgiven? You still love me?" She wrapped her arms and legs around him, thighs wide open in invitation. It felt heavenly. He could never deny her anything when she did this to him. "Now we can have make-up sex. *Oui?* I will let you be on top this time."

He couldn't help but grin like an idiot. "Yes, Michelle, I still love you. I've always loved you. But you knew that already." As they reunited together with the pent-up passions of three nights of abstinence, it didn't escape his notice that Michelle never once mentioned how she felt about him.

* * * *

In bed together, after several rounds of lovingly affectionate sex and mutual biting, Aaron sensed Michelle still had something more to confess.

"Come out with it. There's something else on your mind." He propped himself on his elbows, looking her square in the eyes.

"*Oui.* There is another reason I feared sending you out into the night without my guidance." She paused and caressed his back and thighs, collecting her thoughts. "There is a *problème* I encountered when I was awakened to this life and my control was not very good."

She hesitated. He sensed she was unsure whether or not to continue. She had never spoken of this before, and it had happened so very long ago. He cupped her breast, teasing her nipple with his thumb as he kissed her on the nose. "Please go on. I'd like to hear more."

She nodded and kissed him on the lips while caressing his chest. A very effective distraction. "You know this word *feral?* You know what it means?"

"I think so. It has something to do with a wild animal?"

"*Oui,* is like that. This can happen to us. We are truly predators with instincts to hunt and kill. Vicious killers. When we lose our reason, when we are consumed in strong emotion, is possible to become feral. Is like a mindless wild animal hunting on instinct, attacking anyone who comes near." Michelle paused.

He waited for her to continue. Suddenly her confession seemed very important. He had never considered the ramifications of what she described. But it was all too easy to imagine how it might happen. He had felt a certain *wildness* lurking there inside him recently. It scared him to think such a thing was possible, or that this might have happened to the wonderful creature cuddling with him.

"In France at the end of the war, WWII, something very traumatic happened to me, and I was lost for a time. I roamed the countryside like a wild animal, hunting at night and hiding in basements or holes in the ground by daylight. I don't recall this time very clearly. Is like remembering a dream. I know this can happen to you … if it happened to me." She drew circles on his chest with her fingertips, avoiding direct eye contact. He sensed her embarrassment, she had never admitted this to anyone before.

She must be over eighty years old!

He couldn't fathom this beautiful woman caressing his body roaming across France in the middle of the war. Michelle had never told him anything about her life before they met. He was fascinated to learn more. "Please go on."

"There was a man who found me. Luckily, I did not kill him. I think I was wounded and unconscious, or else I would have attacked him. I spent several weeks with him. In this time I regained my sanity and returned to civilization, after he died. His story is very sad. He died because of me." She paused in solemnity, a powerful sense of regret and loss still there after all those years. She continued, "Someday I will tell you more, but not now."

She looked him in the eyes with her chin on his chest, fingertips stroking his shoulders, and finally got around to the point. "When you came home after your date and I smelled the blood and sex all over you, it brought the memories of this wild life. I became very angry. Because of my assumptions, I wanted to hurt you, as I said before. Also, I was angry with myself. I let you go out without guidance, without an anchor to keep control of the predator. I felt it was my fault you hurt Rosalie."

She paused for a second, considering, then continued. "I was wrong. You did not hurt her. Not really. You have very good control. You cared about this woman." Michelle looked like she was about to cry.

Her vulnerability was arousing. That and her constant stroking up and down his body while she spoke. He rolled her over, pinning her beneath him, and teased her wet entry with his erection, holding her gaze. "You are so damn sexy when you take the blame for me. I'm gonna show you some of that wild animal you're so worried about."

Michelle's eyes popped open wide. She gasped as he buried himself all the way to her core and bit down hard on her neck.

"Ohhh … Aaron … that is *so* wonderful. Give it to me, you animal!"

* * * *

CHAPTER 18

She lay in bed gazing at his sleeping figure. She usually awoke just before sunset, whereas he slept until the sun erased itself completely from the horizon. This allowed her a few moments of solitude to reflect on her new life with this surprisingly wonderful young man.

She so enjoyed watching him sleep. He was truly an enigma to her in so many ways. He was nothing like her former master; virtually every aspect a polar opposite. Where her master had been selfish, sadistic, controlling, manipulative, and vain, Aaron was self-effacing, affectionate, reasonable, and lacked any true arrogance. She had known from their first meeting and the colors of his aura that these mild-mannered traits were inherent to his soul. She never imagined they would carry over with his transformation. She had known he was smitten with her, and she thought it quite noble, his attempt to defend her honor at the hands of the crude detectives.

She supposed his noble intentions contributed to her decision to take his life into her hands. It would have been so much simpler to walk away, leave him bleeding on the concrete. But she knew the odds of surviving such a devastating injury were slim to none. People were so fragile, so easy to kill.

She felt a measure of guilt for his fate. She could easily have disarmed the cop, but she hadn't been concerned for anyone else. She had been taking care of number one, and he was a casualty of her callousness. She had hurt others before in a similar manner, and it still weighed on her conscience to this day. She decided in this one instance she could save a life, instead of allowing death to claim another unfortunate soul. Bringing Aaron into her life, giving him her blood and all that came with it, was a form of atonement for certain wrongs committed in her past.

She now understood she couldn't judge him based on her previous experiences with her master. He simply did not fit her notions of what a male vampire's demeanor and conduct should be. He had been so quick to forgive, and held no residual animosity towards her for the vicious abuse she subjected him to. This was baffling. Why would he forgive her so easily and release all his resentment as though it had never been? The only explanation she could fathom was love. Despite her horrid behavior, he loved her, without reservation. That must be the answer. Nothing else made sense.

It had been worth the risk. Aaron was worth the risk. He was so much more than she ever expected him to be. He filled so many diverse roles in her life. She couldn't imagine living without him. He filled a place in her heart she had not realized was vacant. It was unnerving how strongly she felt for this beautiful boy, her lover, her confidant, her companion. To see him now, contrasted against their first meeting, was like looking at two completely different people. His transformation was magical, like a simple caterpillar that emerges from the cocoon a magnificent butterfly. A creature of beauty and majesty to be marveled at in awe.

She didn't want to admit she might be falling in love with him. A very inconvenient emotion in their tenuous relationship. She couldn't afford to let her feelings override her good sense. Too late, she was already hooked on him.

Never was this more apparent than when she relived his memories of his evening with Rosalie. What he did for the woman was not insignificant. He never really hurt Rosalie. But he did give her a *very* good time, and managed to make her feel loved by a complete stranger. His compassion was amazing. But what shocked Michelle most was Aaron's intense emotions upon returning to her apartment. She experience how he felt about her and her wicked reaction to him, and the events leading up to their horrid lovemaking. These moments twisted Michelle's heart into a tight knot of pain.

He had been so content, anticipating coming home to her. He had a simple and carefree joy, and then she sliced through it, cutting him to the bone, crushing his joy under the heel of her rancor. The hurt she visited on him came back to her tenfold, sending spikes of pain through her heart. Michelle knew this to be the heartache of love. She could no longer deny it or pretend ignorance.

She had fallen in love with her slave.

* * * *

"EZ escort service, how may I help you?"

"Yeah … ah … a friend of mine recommended your agency, said you could arrange an evening with a certain girl."

"Yes of course. Was there a particular girl you had in mind?"

"Yeah … I met her once … she's really unique … a blond with green eyes … her name's Michelle … you know the girl I'm talking about?"

"Oh yes, sir, she's very special indeed. Would you like to schedule a date with her?"

"Yeah, I'm thinking I'd like to see her real soon. Tonight would be good."

"Yes sir. I'm sorry to inform you she won't be available until tomorrow night at 11:00 p.m. Would you like to schedule her then?"

"Tomorrow, uh ... okay. That'll have to do, I guess."

"Certainly. The agency's fee for scheduling with Michelle is one hundred dollars. We can take your credit/debit card over the phone or you can use the payment link in our website. Which would you prefer?"

"A hundred dollars, eh? What's included with that?"

"The agency's scheduling fee is one hundred. Michelle's fee is separate. You will need to bring cash for her. She doesn't accept any other form of payment. Her typical fee is one thousand dollars an hour with a standard two hour minimum, paid in advance."

"Whew! That's pretty steep! That's ... damn!"

"I understand, sir. As you have met Michelle, you know how very special she is, and there's no one like her. Would you prefer to schedule with another girl whose rates are more affordable? I can e-mail you a list with pictures. We have quite a selection to choose from. They are all special in their own way. And quite beautiful, I can assure you."

"No, um ... that's okay ... I'll go ahead and schedule for tomorrow with Michelle. Let's make it the Ramada on Lincoln Boulevard, room three hundred twenty-two. You know where that is?"

"Yes, sir, no problem. I see it now on Google maps. We'll make sure she has the proper directions. Do you have your credit or debit card available to lock in your reservation?"

* * * *

Talco changed Mateo's diaper, working as fast as possible to avoid the *water weenie* effect that happened with uncanny timing—usually as soon as the diaper came off. He had learned after being sprayed several times, the trick was to cover the baby with the new diaper or a towel, anything absorbent. He'd been making good progress when his cell phone buzzed and he used a few precious seconds to retrieve it.

"Los pinche Demonios!" Talco cursed when he saw Konowicz's number on the screen of his phone. At this precise moment, Mateo squealed in laughter, kicked off the towel and shot a stream of lukewarm piss with impeccable aim right at Talco's face. He had read somewhere that urine was a sterilized fluid, but this knowledge didn't help to lessen his revulsion.

Talco felt a creepy sensation tickle down his spine. It was an omen, a portent of bad things to come. And sure enough, Konowicz had left a voicemail directing him to be prepared for Friday night at 10:00 p.m. *Prepared for what? What the hell were they up to now?* Talco knew deep down in his gut, whatever they had planned, it would certainly mean trouble for him. He debated whether or not to call them back. He'd promised Evita not to deal with them anymore, but that was easier said than done.

* * * *

Michelle slipped on her thong panties, teasing Aaron with a flash of pussy as she flipped her dress up with the quick move.

"Damn girl … you are smokin' hot in that dress!" Aaron licked his lips and grabbed her as though planning to drag her back into bed to have his way with her.

"My god, I can barely keep my hands off you! I feel sorry for the sucker who's meeting you tonight. The poor guy never had a chance!"

She wore another variation of the skimpy black cocktail dress that looked so provocative it was probably illegal in certain jurisdictions. Aaron pinned her to the wall stroking her inner thighs, working his warm fingers inside her thong. He didn't mess around, slid right in with two fingers, curving back up to reach the place she liked most. He worked her with such delicious torture that she almost regretted teaching him to hit that spot.

"Ah … Ohhh … Aaron … you will make us both late, you must stop. We both have … We have to go now … Ahh … I'm going … I'm going to get you good tonight. Unghh … ahoof … OH … OH … don't stop now … don't stop! OHHH! *Merde!*"

She came hard in his hand as he stroked her mercilessly. She slumped against him for a moment to catch her breathe, shuddering on his heavenly fingers. She looked up to a proud smirk on his face.

"You naughty, naughty, boy." She wagged her finger playfully at him. "Now I must change."

He sniffed his fingers with that wicked grin as she shut the bedroom door in his face.

In and out of the room quickly, she hoped to catch Aaron before he left, but he was out the door already, headed for his date.

On a whim, she had decided to tell him the truth. She wanted to see the look on his face, to feel his radiant joy as she declared her love for him.

Oh well, it would have to wait.

They certainly had plenty of time; they would be together for many years to come.

On the street out front, Michelle hailed a taxi. "The Ramada Inn, *s'il vous plait.* 1620 Lincoln Boulevard."

* * * *

CHAPTER 19

Aaron stood there silently shocked.

"Hello, Aaron. It's me, Charlene. You remember me, from Bemichis? I hope you don't think it's strange, meeting like this." She hugged his stiff body in greeting.

When he didn't return the gesture, she began wringing her hands, looking a bit nervous. Obviously the tables had turned. She was no longer in a position to assault his derrière with her former confidence.

"I caught your pictures the other day in the weekly e-mail from EZ Escorts and I knew I just had to see you. I hope you don't mind."

He was surprised to say the least, but not in a bad way. Though he'd never really considered sex with Charlene, he actually liked her.

He smiled and put her at ease. "I've always thought it would be fun to get better acquainted. I'm glad we got a chance to meet casually away from Bemichis. It would've been inappropriate to see each other like this if I was still working there." Bemichis repeated warnings about fraternizing with customers still rang clearly in his mind, etched into permanent memory. "So … what did you have in mind for this evening?"

"I thought we could skip all the bullshit and head on up to the room …" He followed Charlene's imagination as she pictured sequences of hot passionate sex involving champagne, strawberries, and Aaron naked in the Jacuzzi. He plucked the ideas from her mind and suggested the very thing she fantasized about.

"Strawberries, champagne, and a hot bath?"

His suggestion rendered her speechless. She gazed into his eyes, giddy with the happiness of a child on Christmas day. He held her securely in his embrace as they made their way to the elevator.

In the hotel room he ordered room service while Charlene settled on a top forties music channel and watched him with more than a little anticipation. Her face flushed as she hoped he would rub her down in a sensual massage.

Seemed like a good idea to him. "I bet you could use a good back rub." He slid on the bed behind her, his legs straddling her hips, and began rubbing her shoulders and back. She tensed up for a moment, and then melted into his caress.

He took time to appreciate Charlene's beauty as he undid the clip of her bra. Creamy white skin and wavy, auburn hair reached down to the center of her back. Her body curved in all the right places with generous hips and breasts. A hint of extra weight around the middle, but still quite attractive. She didn't need to pay for dates. She could pick up men anytime she wanted. Her problem was she preferred a young boy-toy who could match her voracious sexual appetite. Charlene also had two teen-age boys at home. Not a situation conductive to finding and keeping a good man.

Charlene's mind drifted to the places she wanted his touch, her nipples and the nape of her neck. Her mind created the road map for her sensual massage. He followed her vivid imagination and began working her full breasts, tweaking her nipples while nipping at her neck and ear lobes with light kisses. Her arousal ramped up quickly, each touch wetting her in anticipation.

She wanted his fingers down inside her, rubbing and dipping into her moist, ready folds. He followed her lead and reached his hand to pull up her dress, baring her thighs. His palm caressed her shaved pubic flesh while curling his middle finger into her wetness. She grasped his hand and directed his movements, grinding her hips. She worked herself to a frenzy with his fingers deep in her wet center.

Charlene bucked and moaned. "Unh ... Unh ... Ooooohh ... Yes!" A sunburst of her pleasure exploded in his mind as she wetted his hand with her climax.

She finished right on time. Room service knocked at the door to announce the arrival of the champagne and strawberries. Aaron tended to the cart, setting it up by the bath. Charlene caught her breath and then ran the bath, undressing without ceremony. She wasn't modest. She had no fear of displaying her well-proportioned body.

The tub was a one piece fiberglass unit with air jets, a Jacuzzi just large enough for the two of them. Charlene slid into the tub with a sigh of pleasure. Leaning back with a smile, her creamy white breasts floated at the waterline. She caught him appreciating her body and winked.

He handed her a glass of champagne and she downed it all at once. She invited in a seductive whisper. "Come on in, the water's warm and ready."

He looked at her with an inward smile. *Un huh. And the water's not the only thing warm and ready.* He could see her arm moving as she played with herself beneath the bubbles.

As he undressed, he read her desire to taste his cock. *Don't want to disappoint.*

He accommodated her standing at the edge of the tub with his erection beckoning to her. Charlene tossed back her second glass of champagne, leaned forward, and swallowed him whole. She pumped his base while sucking hard and fast. The woman knew what she was doing. She slid up and down his cock, moving her hand along its length as she suckled on the very tip. She got down on it, alternating from full-on deep throat to intense tongue, lips, and teeth action on the sensitive head of his cock. In no time at all he lost control. He shot straight into her suction as she milked him dry, working out every last drop she could squeeze. He gripped her hair shoving all the way back down her throat with his climax.

After letting Charlene catch her breath, he climbed into the tub facing her. She wiped her mouth off and went to work on a third glass of champagne. She attempted to get him to join her, but instead he fed her strawberries while she knocked back her third and fourth glasses of Dom Pérignon.

Charlene was drunk as a skunk and having a blast. "Well don't just sit there looking pretty with all that cock. Give me that monster."

She reached out to take him in hand. In no time at all she tugged him back up to full size. With one smooth move she expertly mounted him. Her hot, tight cunt seated all the way down. Her legs out to each side—she ground down, rotating her hips back and forth, holding the side of the tub while stroking herself with the other hand.

His preternatural strength allowed him to pound and grind forcefully with an iron grip on her generous thighs. His powerful thrusts and her own playful hands brought her to the edge quickly.

Charlene reached came hard, crying out her pleasure in sexy little moans. He chose this moment to strike, burying his teeth in her neck while she humped him for all she was worth. He drank deeply, hitting that familiar domino effect of multiple, cascading orgasms. Charlene screamed and cried with the force of her repeated climaxes. Buried to the hilt, he came deep inside her, and released his bite. Charlene's body had become liquid flesh, vibrating and quivering, unable to support herself. She heaved and gasped, making weird grunt noises, crying. It had been one hell of an intense ride for the middle-aged mother of two. He stood up in the bath with her in his arms, still impaled. She was too drunk and dazed to take notice of his uncommon strength.

He carried her from the bath. Every step he took brought a sweet wine from her lips, as she bounced on his cock. He laid her on the bed and carefully slid out from between her legs.

"Or lord." She sighed and twitched as he pulled out.

He dreaded what he might find. Much to his relief she wasn't bleeding. He didn't know how common it was that women might bleed from a good hard pounding, but he definitely didn't want to make a habit of it. He tucked her into bed and kissed her tenderly. Her exhaustion and intoxication dragged her down into unconsciousness. She smiled up at him with her venom-alcohol glazed eyes and slurred, "This is the best date I've ever had! Where were you twenty years ago?"

In my mother's belly.

She passed out dead asleep with a slobbering half-smile pasted on her face. He dressed and headed out the door. Luckily, Charlene arranged for a thousand dollar prepayment for her two hour date through the agency's merchant account. The woman was out cold, not waking up anytime soon. He felt a fleeting twinge of guilt for having shorted her on the time, but she got her money's worth. No harm, no foul.

✴ ✴ ✴ ✴

CHAPTER 20

Michelle made a stop at the mall to browse for some beauty products and found a couple pairs of sheer G-strings to purchase for her next adventure with Aaron —*scheduled for about 3 hours from now*. She caught another taxi, arriving at the Ramada Inn at exactly eleven o'clock, right on time.

As she knocked on the door to Room 322, she hoped this wouldn't be another disgusting politician. How nice it would be to spend her evening meeting someone enjoyable for a change. The man who answered the door seemed out of place. He didn't fit the profile of the aging wealthy clients she usually dealt with. His young, fit, Latin looks and accent were too attractive. Why would he pay a thousand dollars an hour for a couple hours of fun when he could pick-up most women in a night club? He carried himself with assurance and confidence. Not the type who needed to pay for a woman's attentions.

He introduced himself as Talco. Her finely honed instincts sensed something wrong. He didn't follow her properly into the room. Instead he closed the door, locked it behind him, and remained where he stood. She stretched her senses, trying to smell, taste, hear, or feel what it was that had put her on the defensive. She heard two heartbeats and respirations in a nearby room, but nothing she could put her finger on as the source of her anxiety.

She turned around to study Talco. His aura exhibited the coloration of nervousness and anticipation—a fairly normal set of emotions for clients awaiting a prostitute. She noticed he had a hint of something else, like the caged aggression of a boxer preparing to enter the ring. He seemed to be guarding the door. By the time she realized that's exactly what he was doing, it was too late.

Suddenly the side door leading to the adjoining room slammed open, and the two detectives she'd confronted two weeks earlier marched into the room. The look of recognition and satisfaction on their faces spoke volumes.

She turned whip-fast towards Talco and the door, but he was prepared for her with a Taser in hand. She surveyed the room for another possible exit and noticed both cops also had Tasers drawn and held in ready position.

She studied the unwholesome lust for violence and vengeance displayed in the detective's auras. They lacked any of the benevolence found in decent law enforcement officials. This was not an arrest related to police business. This was premeditated murder.

As she considered her options she realized she was no longer alone in the world to face such dangers. She reached out to Aaron through the channel of their psychic bond and beamed a powerful directive: COME NOW! I NEED YOU! I'M TRAPPED!

With the confidence Aaron was on his way, she debated against waiting for him or taking extreme action alone. She preferred not to give the police a chance to do anything preemptive. She needed to do something to buy time for Aaron to arrive. She would take her chances and fight her way out.

She leaped at Talco, gaining speed and force to take him out. Luck was with him. His Taser fired into her chest at the last second, instantly dropping her to the floor. She'd never been tasered before. It was a new lesson in pain. She hit the carpet jerking in extreme agony, all her nerve endings firing. Her muscles seized up tight as 50,000 volts screamed through her nervous system. Talco kept the Taser engaged non-stop until one of the cops yelled, "Enough! She's toast already!"

Immobile on the floor, but still conscious, she caught a quick breath, and slammed up into Talco, throwing him across the room to smash against the wall. She was three feet from the door when the detectives hit her simultaneously in the back with both their Tasers.

They held the juice to her non-stop while Talco recovered and joined them for the combined effect of three different electric charges hitting her in unison. The white-hot pain of electric shock blotted out her world.

* * * *

Aaron stood on the roof of the apartment building he called home, looking out over the city, breathing in the aromatic night air. He recalled that first night, when Michelle forced him to jump. He'd resisted her at every step, but the changes she brought to his life couldn't be undone. He wouldn't have it any other way, for better or worse, he was committed to making this work out between them. That's when it hit him.

A jolt of intense NEED from Michelle smacked his psyche, knocking him to the ground with its power. He heard her scream as though she were standing next to him. His being was possessed with the overpowering compulsion to reach Michelle NOW. She was about twenty miles away on the third floor of a hotel.

He was up and running in an instant, rapid fire. He hit the edge of the building and jumped with every last ounce of strength, flying across to the other building. He hit the ground running and kept on going, leaping from rooftop to rooftop until he reached a building extending ten stories above his level. Without pause he turned and barreled towards the main street, flowing in the direction of the hotel. He leapt down from the roof to a lower corner store and then down onto the street.

His mind raced through scenarios, imagining what could be wrong, galvanized with fear for her wellbeing. With his mind opened wide to their bond, he felt the blinding agony of excruciating electric shock. He staggered, going down on all fours in a haze of pain. He was dizzy, nauseous, it was too much. He couldn't help her and share her pain at the same time. He reeled his mind back from Michelle and blocked himself into his mental vault.

With a clear head and a renewed sense of urgency, he jumped up and raced down the street, picking up speed, leaping across intersections, careening off moving vehicles. He vaulted off parked cars and dodged left and right as he negotiated the obstacles in the streets and sidewalks. In his urgency, he moved heedless of who might witness him and remark on such super-human displays of speed.

* * * *

Michelle awoke to throbbing waves of pain lashing across her entire body. Every limb, all her fingers and toes, every single hair on her head, every molecule in her body, radiated nauseating pain. She heard cursing in Brooklyn accents interspersed with Talco's exclamations in a mixture of Spanish and English, then the click-snap of Taser cartridges reloaded. Time to drag her sorry ass off the floor and do something.

She suddenly spun on the ground kicking out in all directions. She was lucky enough to catch someone in the knee, knocking him down. With a target acquired, she kicked out again, hard in his groin. She scrambled up and over his body to grasp his weapon. As she turned toward the other cop, Taser in hand, the fat bastard had his gun drawn. He fired three shots point blank, piercing her right shoulder, and throwing her against the wall where she slumped to the floor.

She lay there in shock and disbelief, bleeding out all her precious blood onto the hotel carpet. She was closer to death than she'd been in decades. She reached out to Aaron with a desperate psychic cry, screaming with all her consciousness for him to save her life. A few seconds everything faded to black.

* * * *

Vertigo punched him viciously. He stumbled to a halt, falling in a tumble across the sidewalk as the psychic backlash hit him with a tsunami of Michelle's desperation tearing through his mind. The force of her desperate need delved deep into his psyche, unhinging logic and reason. A primeval consciousness took over Aaron's mind and a massive adrenaline high slammed him into extreme overdrive.

He screamed into the night, a blood curdling sound of bottomless rage. He rocketed down the street, a blur of movement. The unchained Predator knew instinctively there were too many obstacles on the street, too many people with their complications. He leaped to the side of the nearest building, bounding upward to catch the lip of the brick at each window, defying gravity and gaining momentum. Reaching the top in seconds, he leaped across to the next building's roof, soaring from building to building, a streak of black lightning across the skyline. The Predator preferred the high ground for strategic hunting advantage and a better view of the target.

The Predator reached the Ramada Inn within moments. He sailed through the window of an unoccupied third floor room. He landed in the center of the room, flowing with his momentum. He smashed through the door into the hallway and barreled towards Room 322.

* * * *

CHAPTER 21

Talco knew a mess when he saw one. "I'm fuckin' outta here! I don't know what kinda drugs that bitch is on, and I don't care. I'm not getting dragged into a homicide investigation. You're on your own!" Stepping into the hallway, he came face to face with a demon from hell sent to collect his due. He had waited a moment too long to make his exit, and the time had come to answer for his sins. The last conscious thought echoing through Talco's mind was the beginnings of the *Our Father* prayer. He never made it past *who art in heaven.*

* * * *

The Predator read Talco's shock and anxiety at having witnessed Michelle's execution. He could see the gruesome image in Talco's mind as he made the grave mistake of stepping directly into the Predator's path. He plowed right through the man, hitting Talco with a crushing blow to his chest, slamming him into the wall at the end of the hallway. He rendered Talco unconscious in one move.

As he tore the door off the hinges to Room 322, the Predator read the detective's minds revealing their premeditated attack on Michelle. Their scheme had unraveled fast. They were forced to shoot her here in the hotel instead of disposing of her in the back alley as planned.

The detectives must die.

There would be none of the mercy given to Talco. Moving in slow motion, they telegraphed their intent to draw down on him with their firearms. He moved wicked fast, smashing Oberman in the chest. Oberman sailed through the air backward, exploding the sliding glass door and flying over the balcony into the parking lot below. It happened so fast that to the unaided human eye it seemed the Predator teleported into place where Oberman was standing.

The Predator slipped into position as though filling Oberman's vacuum. In a sweeping arc of his claws, he swiped the flesh from Konowicz's throat like a hot knife carving through butter.

The Predator latched onto the gaping wound, guzzling down Konowicz's life blood as it sprayed and gushed from his body. He drank his fill, engorging himself until there was no fluid left to consume. He flung the limp, lifeless sack of flesh to the ground and retrieved Michelle's blood-soaked body cradling her to his chest.

He had dispatched all three men in under five seconds flat, threats neutralized. The stench of blood was overpowering, calling him to feed. All that adrenaline, all that bottomless rage and power, and now what? He burned to kill, to rend and tear flesh, to crush bones, to devour the cattle herding in the streets below. He could smell, hear, and taste their idle flesh there at the edge of his senses as they went about their meaningless pursuits. It would be all too easy. No one could stop him from feasting on their bloated, fattened bodies.

A more urgent instinct begged his attention. His master lay in his arms helpless. He smelled and sensed her impending death. She needed sanctuary. She had been wounded to the very limits of her miraculous healing capacity and perhaps beyond. Holding Michelle securely in his arms, he fled to seek a refuge against the coming daylight.

* * * *

Michelle's basest survival instincts brought her awake to the smell of blood. Her body's primal need for precious life-giving blood to regenerate and heal overwhelmed all other conscious thought. She sensed the blood and flesh wrapped around her, and tore into it with ravenous hunger. The flesh fought her. It was too strong, too powerful, denying her the blood that she needed so badly. She instinctively knew she could force it into submission with her words. In her overwhelming need, without cognizance of her actions, Michelle commanded, "Be Still!"

She tore into the flesh and drank deeply from its jugular vein.

* * * *

Michelle awoke in an abandoned building, her arms and legs intimately wrapped around Aaron, who lie on his back beneath her. Her face was buried in his neck. They were both covered in icky-sticky caked blood. She could not recall any details beyond the gunshots fired in the hotel room. Her thirst was intense, but she fought the urge to bite him. She was unsure of his condition. Upon further inspection she saw his ragged clothing hung in tattered shreds. He looked as though he'd been to Hell and back again, fought off a pack of wild animals. Much the worse for it.

She was very sore. Her chest, ribs, shoulder, collar bone, neck, back, and basically her whole upper body ached and throbbed in pain. Her clothes looked like Aaron's—shredded. She must've fought someone with a blade. Her gunshot wounds were mostly healed. The scabs flaked loose to reveal the pinkish marks of freshly-healed skin beneath the caked blood. And there were marks revealing recent wounds of some other kind. She couldn't recall having fought with anyone besides the detectives, no one with a blade that would do this kind of damage. A thought came to her then, but she dismissed it immediately.

Aaron would never attack her.

With the growing intensity of her hunger, her senses magnified to encompass the surrounding area and streets outside. She smelled the ripe bodily stench of unwashed vagrants. She arose and fed ungracefully from the two squatters living in the upper levels of the abandoned building. They were both dazed and stupefied from the raw force of her animalistic feeding. She left them where they lay, still alive, and returned to Aaron.

The sun had dropped below the horizon an hour ago, and yet he did not rise. She felt vulnerable out in the city. She was unsure of the final outcome with the police last night. She scooped Aaron to her and carried him home. It took an hour to reach her apartment as she moved steadily and cautiously through the alleyways, taking great care to avoid being seen in their blood-drenched, alarming appearance.

She toweled Aaron off then bathed herself and waited for him to arise. By ten p.m., three hours after sunset, she became panic-stricken. She decided to feed him her blood. She could think of nothing else to help him. She cut her wrist and placed it to his mouth. He didn't move, didn't react like he should have. She rubbed it around on his lips and nose, smearing it all over, tempting him to feed.

At the point where she thought for sure something was seriously wrong, he reacted, clamping his hands around her arm as he sunk his fangs in deep. A violent chomp. His jaw locked down with painful force, digging his canines in all the way to the bone. The wonderful side-effects of his venom helped offset the pain of his violent response. As usual, his venom packed a wallop, heating her erogenous zones and bringing her to a toe-curling orgasm. She warmed to it, panting hard and fast as he brought her to a peak and kept on going. When she had climaxed twice and began to feel lightheaded from blood loss, she commanded him to STOP. It took her a moment to catch her breath. Her head spun from the intense experience.

She lay atop his naked body on the bed looking into his eyes, searching for a sign he was in there somewhere. He appeared cognizant. He seemed aware of her as he held her gaze.

"Aaron can you understand me ... Talk to me please." She desperately needed to hear his voice.

He could barely speak in a hoarse, croaked reply. "Unghh ... my throat really hurts. You bit me hard last night. How are you? You were in really bad shape. I wasn't sure if you'd make it."

"*Mon dieu*, I was so worried. You were so still. I was afraid ..."

She smiled a huge fang-filled grin and hugged him close, kissing him full on the lips. "I am fine. Really. My dress is completely ruined, and my shoulder still hurts, but the wounds are mostly healed." She smiled at him with embarrassment, rubbing her shoulder and moving her arm in a circular motion.

"Aaron ... what happened to the policemen?" She pulled her blonde curls behind her ear and shifted her legs as she straddled him, sitting up halfway.

"I'm not really sure. It's kinda fuzzy, like a dream. It might be easier to show you."

Michelle accepted his invitation, delving into his mind as he opened wide to their psychic bond and recalled all the events of the night before. She relived, with him, the harrowing race through the streets to make his way to the hotel. He was so damn powerful and he moved so fast it was disorienting. She went along for the ride through his attack on the detectives, reveling in their slaughter and the wondrous sensation of draining every last drop of Konowicz's blood.

She flew through the night with him as he raced across the rooftops, her own body in his arms, seeking refuge. In the basement of the abandoned building she tasted her own blood as he licked her wounds to help cleanse and stop the bleeding. And then she lived through the most vicious fight she'd ever been in. Aaron fought for his life against a crazed, half-dead vampire driven insane with the need for blood.

He was winning the battle. He clawed, scraped and gouged at the lunatic beast in his arms trying to get at his throat. Then she used her power of compulsion to hold him still while she tore out his jugular vein and satiated herself on his blood. She was there with him till the moment he passed into unconsciousness from blood loss and the trauma of her unrestrained assault. She felt how he sensed his own death was near, but was unable to save himself for the power she held over him.

Michelle cried out. She collapsed onto his chest, tears of blood streaming down her face. "*Ah, la vache!* Oh Aaron, please forgive me. I was not aware. I didn't know what I was doing!"

She buried her face in his chest, unable to look him in the eyes, and sobbed from the unwanted memories of all the horror and trauma she put him through. He held her, stroked her hair and shushed her, offering comfort for her misery.

"I would never hurt you like that on purpose." She looked up, pleading with her eyes for understanding.

But she could no longer deny the truth. She had tried to kill him, and it wasn't the first time. She had done it before when she'd attacked him in the middle of their lovemaking. It was the luck of the draw and his powerful vampire physique that allowed him to survive.

Despite all that she had done, he wasn't angry, he forgave her. She never had to ask forgiveness. It had already been given. He loved her too much to stay angry.

It poured out without thought. She blurted it out, unable to hold back the powerful well of emotion, "I love you Aaron. I need you. I need you to love me. Say it … tell me how much you love me." She clung to him in desperation.

"I love you, Michelle, and I would give you my life if you asked for it." His mind still wide open, she knew the truth of his words. She need not fight for his blood. He'd have given it to her willingly, if she asked.

She kissed him with a need so powerful and all-consuming it was unbearable.

* * * *

Aaron kissed her back, holding her tightly as he rolled her over, pinning her beneath him with an unbreakable grip. He stopped his frantic kissing only long enough to sink his fangs into her neck with love and passion as he entered her slowly, gradually filing her womb with his engorged cock. Being in love was the biggest turn-on he'd ever known. Buried deep inside her, he released his bite and looked her in the eyes, "Say it again!"

He pinned her arms above her head and trapped her beneath him, her robe wide open exposing her breasts. With a shift of his weight he slammed in deep to her core.

She gasped in surprise, a spark of fear in her eyes. He had her trapped. She couldn't move unless he allowed it. With tears of blood welling in her eyes she cried, "Aaron, I beg you, please forgive me! I'm sorry I hurt you!"

"No, you silly woman, tell me again that you love me! I want to hear you say it over and over!"

He thrust into her moist heat faster and faster frantically making love to her as she cried out repeatedly, "I love you! I love you!"

He pounded her relentlessly, going at it with a vigor that shouldn't exist in a man who had almost died several hours ago.

"*Je t'aime Aaron! Mon amour pour toi est éternel!*"

She drove him mad with her guttural cries of eternal love. They tumbled and rolled over and over, off the bed, across the floor, up against the wall, atop the dresser, smashing the vanity mirror. Like animals they grunted and growled their way to an explosive peak. "*Ahhh plus! plus! plus!*" She cried out for more.

They orgasmed together, biting over and over, and eventually collapsed onto the floor in a heap of twisted limbs.

She stroked him all over his arms and shoulders purring into his ear. "I will always love you Aaron. I want you so much. *J'ai envie de toi.*"

Her proclamation of eternal love filled him with indescribable joy. Her mind was wide open to their bond, her love pouring over him like a wondrous fountain of light. He had attained nirvana. His universe aligned perfectly with the knowledge that their love was mutual.

A great weight lifted from his shoulders, a burden he hadn't realized was there. He felt invincible. The whole world was his for the taking, as long as she remained at his side.

* * * *

Michelle meditated upon her new life with its confusion of contradictory feelings. She hadn't experienced such turmoil of emotion since all those years ago in France. It seemed a lifetime ago. She felt terrified by the uninhibited violence Aaron displayed at the hotel. And more than a little intimidated by the phenomenal physical superiority he demonstrated in those adrenaline-soaked adventures flying through the city at incredible velocity. It had been like entering the mind and body of a wild animal on rampage, but with the added boost of unnatural strength.

Michelle had never imagined how powerful the unchained beast lurking inside Aaron truly was. He could have taken on an army of soldiers. He could definitely take her.

In spite of her shock, she felt a wellspring of love and ecstatic joy. He was alive after all he had been through. His humanity and purity of spirit seemed untainted by those horrid experiences. Michelle felt an indescribable happiness at having the miracle of Aaron in her life. She feared she didn't deserve such a blessing. His only care upon waking from the massacre of the night before was for her wellbeing. He didn't even fault her for trying to kill him—and damn near succeeding.

For the first time in many, many years, Michelle felt secure and safe. She was no longer alone in this cold, harsh world. She had a mate, a companion, a protector, a vicious warrior to fight her battles. She truly loved him for all that he was, and more importantly, all that he wasn't. The aching loneliness of her solitary nightlife had been replaced with a radiant and wonderful existence. He supplied her life with a vital, missing ingredient, that *'je ne sais quoi'*, an indescribable something special. A *'raison d'être'*, a reason for being.

* * * *

CHAPTER 21

As the nights flowed past without incident following the Ramada Inn massacre, Aaron became aware of a new presence co-existing within his psyche, an aggressive, violent personality he dubbed *the Predator*. The Predator lurked there just below the surface of his mind, waiting. Aaron knew this was the entity that had possessed his faculties, his mind and body, during the attack on the detectives. He recognized this elusive thing within was simply a much baser, primitive part of his own mind.

The Predator watched people, perusing through their thoughts, intentions, and movements, a semi-conscious surveillance system keeping tabs on every detail of his waking life. The Predator made constant assessments out the corner of Aaron's eyes, checking the exits, watching his back, keeping vigil for any potential threat.

The Predator seemed to have its own set of emotions apart from Aaron's. It functioned with a baser, more primitive reaction to people, places, things, involving urges to fight, defend, attack, feed, or to simply enjoy the pleasure of moving at fantastic speeds through the night air, rejoicing in its agility and prowess.

At times the Predator drifted a little closer to the surface of his mind, pushing its aggressive agenda over the top of Aaron's thought processes. This was rare, but almost predictable. It was always precipitated by some situation where the Predator perceived a threat. At first Aaron didn't even realize these baser urges of aggression were not truly his own.

In these moments where his control over the beast slipped, it sometimes acted of its own will, enslaving Aaron's body to its desires. In one instance, it almost killed a man. It happened while running an errand for Michelle. She sent Aaron to the corner store a couple blocks down the street. As he walked along minding his own business, a hapless bum hobbled out of the alleyway. He probably intended to ask for spare change or whatever. The Predator saw a threat. Before Aaron knew what happened, the Predator leaped forward, seizing his motor skills. He lashed out at the vagrant with a back hand, knocking the poor guy sprawling across the sidewalk.

Aaron stood in complete shock and awe at what he'd done. The vagrant cursed and spit at him in a toothless garble, "Ga dern sumbitch. Leavemee lone! I ain't touch you. Don't go messin' with me, ya crazy bastard!"

He stood there gawking at the filthy old geezer like an idiot. The man picked himself up and limped off, cursing the whole way. Since that incident Aaron realized he'd have to maintain a vigil of his own, to keep a close eye on the Predator's reactions and urges, keep it from bleeding over into his life.

The Predator knew otherwise. It knew there would always be those incidents—*moments of need*—when decisive, aggressive action would be necessary. Like a caged lion that *knows* it will escape eventually, the Predator waited patiently for Aaron to leave the door unlatched.

* * * *

Michelle noticed the change in Aaron immediately. He was now a man in every sense of the word. There was a rock-solid powerful presence beneath every movement and expression. His carriage, stance, demeanor, walk, everything about him spoke of power. The kind of inner strength that comes with being self-assured of the ability to manage any situation.

Without words to acknowledge the event, their relationship had completely morphed overnight. He became her equal. There was no more of the motherly mentorship role. Aaron's judgment, instincts, capabilities, and maturity were unquestionable. She had nothing left to teach that he hadn't learned that night.

She loathed using her authority of compulsion for any reason other than a dire life-threatening emergency. It seemed an offensive act to degrade this powerful, graceful creature with a compulsive command.

Like a person who owns a wild animal, to taunt the beast with cruel treatment is to risk loss of life and limb. She didn't wish to arouse Aaron's wrath with petty commands of compulsion. He was a force to be reckoned with, not manipulated. To this extent, she actually feared him. Without the reassurance of his love, without his constant affection, she'd be looking over her shoulder for a stab in the back.

She understood, probably better than Aaron did, exactly how vicious and dangerous a male vampire could be. She had no desire to evoke the darkness within him. He was normally the perfect vision of comportment and civility, and she wanted to keep it that way.

Their relationship functioned on a new paradigm of mutual love and respect. But she was no longer his master. Not if she valued her life. Her days of ordering Aaron around were finished.

* * * *

MEDICAL EXAMINER RULES N.Y.P.D.
DETECTIVES DEATHS A DOUBLE HOMICIDE

The death of fifty-two year old detective Conner Oberman with the 124th precinct N.Y.P.D., has been ruled a homicide, the medical examiner's office said Monday. Detective Oberman was found face-down in the south side parking lot of the Ramada Inn on Lincoln Blvd. at 11:55 p.m. Friday evening by police officials responding to reports of multiple gunshots fired. Investigators determined that Oberman fell to his death from the third floor balcony of room 322.

In a related homicide, Oberman's partner, forty-nine year old Detective Sean Konowicz with the 124th precinct N.Y.P.D., was pronounced dead at the scene in room 322 of the same hotel. Detective Konowicz's autopsy states, "… massive trauma to the trachea …" with a "… significant contributing factor of external hemorrhage as the cause of death," according to the news release from the medical examiner's office. When asked if the detectives were on official police business when the murders took place, Police Chief Schueller declined to comment stating, "The investigation is ongoing and the N.Y.P.D. homicide detectives are following all potential leads." There have been no suspects identified as of yet and no new developments in the investigation beyond the medical examiner's reports.

CHAPTER 22

Michelle handed her cell phone off to Aaron. "Is your friend again. Please make the arrangements." He nodded and winked at her.

"Hey Kyle, it's good to hear from you. What's up?"

"Same ole same ole. What have you been doing with yourself lately? Seems like forever since we hung out." Kyle hadn't spoken to him in over a week. Not since he called to warn him about the detectives.

"I'm doing great, fantastic actually. I've been keeping really busy. Michelle's got me running here, there, and everywhere." Aaron snorted at the inside joke.

"I'll bet. You gotta do whatever it takes to keep a girl like Michelle happy." Obviously Kyle was still enthralled with Michelle, but then who wasn't? Everyone she came into contact with fell under her spell. She collected admirers like other women collect shoes.

"You betcha. I make sure to do everything I can to keep my baby happy. You wouldn't want to see what she's like when she's angry. That's something to avoid at all costs." Aaron paused and then redirected, "How about you? What's new? Find a new roommate yet?"

"No man, I guess I'm just a sentimental fool. I can't bring myself to put anyone else in your room. It wouldn't be the same." Kyle spoke as though reciting a Shakespearean tragedy.

"Stop it. You're gonna make me cry!" Aaron mimicked Kyle's tragic tone. He knew the truth—Kyle simply couldn't find another chump to foot the bill for half the rent and utilities.

"Hey, man, don't get all weepy on me. You know I can't handle it. Really, I called to invite you and Michelle to a little party I'm having this Friday. Since you can't seem to find the time to come see your best friend I decided to throw a party. Seemed like a good excuse to get you to show up."

"*Ohhh reeaaallly.* And should I assume this invitation comes with the requirement that I bring a twenty-four pack?"

Kyle snickered. "You know me far too well. It's like you can read my mind or somethin'. Kinda startin' to creep me out dude!"

"I tell you what, I'll make you a deal. I'll show up with a twenty-four pack and my fabulously gorgeous girlfriend, ready to party, on one condition … You make sure Delia's there."

"You got it, man. She woulda been here anyway. You know that." Kyle paused. "I gotta say, Michelle has Delia beat hands down, all the way around. It's like, no contest. Honestly, I don't know why you'd be interested in Delia anymore."

"Definitely, Michelle is awesome, no doubt about it. But hey ... don't say anything to Delia about this, okay? I want to surprise her. Got it?"

"Sure, no problem, catch you Friday, around ten. You take care. Tell Michelle I said hi." Kyle hung up.

Aaron turned to Michelle with a wicked smile that didn't quite reach his eyes, "Hey, baby, we're goin' to a party Friday night! Delia's gonna be there. Make sure you let her know how much we appreciate everything she's done for us."

"*Oui mon chéri*, I will make sure she knows exactly how I feel!"

* * * *

Talco felt like he truly had a guardian angel. Someone up above had taken pity on him. He'd been delivered from the hands of the demon who came to drag Oberman and Konowicz to Hell. Sure he had some broken ribs, and a surgery on his punctured lung, but he was alive and well, relatively speaking. Sitting in his hospital bed, he read the newspaper daily, searching for any mention of the detectives. He saw the articles, which said very little, but it was enough.

He knew the score. He knew how very close he came to sharing their fate. It was divine intervention that woke him from unconsciousness in the hotel hallway and steered him down the stairwell to life and freedom. His escape from the Ramada Inn was nothing short of a religious experience.

The police didn't have a clue he had been there. There were no witnesses who survived. What could a witness testify to anyway? Would a judge and jury listen to tales of demonic entities sent to collect the damned, dragging their souls down into the abyss? There was no way to explain to the faithless what had occurred that night.

He swore to bury the memory. None would ever hear his tale. He'd keep this event close to his chest and build upon it a foundation for a new life free of corruption. He would be a good father, a good husband, a good member of the church and community.

His deal with the devil had been broken, his life spared. He would not waste this opportunity to remake himself in the eyes of God and all those he loved.

* * * *

Aaron smiled wide as Kyle opened the door to his apartment.

"Hey Aaron, my man, my savior, what would I do without you—and your beer?" Kyle bumped knuckles with him and then took in Michelle in all her splendor. "Ah Michelle, mon amour, you're looking lovely as ever." Kyle made eyes at her, grabbing her hand as though he would kiss it. She swatted him away and smiled demurely, in character with her girl-next-door persona, assumed and discarded at the flick of a switch.

Michelle did indeed look lovely in her second-skin, black jeans and skimpy, red top with lots of open back and cleavage.

Aaron saw Delia immediately, camped on the other side of the room with Amber and gang. Delia could not stop staring at him. He acted like she didn't exist.

As the party raged on, he and Michelle worked the room, enjoying the carefree light-hearted atmosphere of the young, immature party goers. Delia was completely ignored, but she maintained her relentless stare at Aaron. Reading her mind, she was consumed with jealousy, obsessed with him, desperately waiting for an opening to talk with him alone. Michelle had been right all along, the girl was a problem.

A half hour into the party, Amber approached him. "Can I talk to you for a second?" Her eyes flitted to Michelle, who was occupied with Kyle's flirtations.

"I'm right here." He smiled brightly, and she blushed.

He read Amber's intense attraction to him and her embarrassment at being cornered into the awkward position of acting as Delia's ambassador. He listened patiently. "Um ... really its Delia, she wants to talk privately, in the bedroom. She really misses you. I mean it. I've never seen her like this. Can you just talk to her for a couple minutes?" Amber's eyes shifted back towards Michelle, as though afraid to be caught in the middle of this little game.

He surprised her with a wide open grin. "Yeah, let's do it."

Aaron flashed a winning smile in Delia's direction. The first time he'd given her any attention all night. She blushed too. He wondered if Delia had a clue how much her best friend wanted to get in his pants. She probably wouldn't be sending Amber to him anymore if she learned the truth.

He drew Delia into the room, putting his arm around her in a casual embrace as he closed the door behind them. Delia's pulse pounded and he read her intense desire-obsession, as she grew wet between the legs from his proximity. She knew something exciting was about to happen. She couldn't understand what had come over her. He had never driven her hormones crazy like this. No man had ever affected her this way.

He pulled away from her and stepped farther into the bedroom. The separation was almost painful for Delia. She yearned to touch him, to reach her hands up under his shirt. She broke into a sweat with fantasies of all the delightfully naughty things she wanted him to do.

He stood there looking at her. Gradually his face turned to a scowl, eyes cold as ice. Delia began to fear he had discovered she called the police to report Michelle. She feared his disapproval and rejection. Her mind raced through lies, misdirection and excuses she could use to skirt the issue, preparing for a reproach.

He read her as she unwittingly confessed to her betrayal that led to the Ramada Inn massacre and his and Michelle's near-death-experiences. Delia had just condemned herself. The judge, jury, and executioner stood right behind her, silently reading all that Aaron discovered through their intimate psychic bond. Michelle had slipped into the room silently after them, and stood directly behind Delia the entire time. He transmitted all of Delia's thoughts to her.

Sensing something was seriously wrong, Delia began blabbering nervously, "I have done a lot of thinking lately, and I realize I was wrong about splitting up. You know we belong together." She smiled warmly with an air of correctness and expectation, no hint of innocence or apology.

Aaron walked toward Delia as though he would embrace her again, but kept on going right past her. As she turned to grab him, he walked into Michelle's embrace and kissed her lovingly.

Michelle broke off and patted him gently on the shoulder. "Delia and I have something to discuss. Give us a moment, please."

He nodded and quickly exited the room, closing the door behind him.

* * * *

Delia tried to follow Aaron out, moving past Michelle towards the door. Michelle snatched her up off her feet one-handed, spun her around and pinned her back to the door, face to face. She had Delia by the throat, pressed securely against the door with her feet dangling in the air. Delia squirmed frantically, trying to somehow free herself from the iron claws that dug into her throat like a bear trap.

Michelle's mouth opened inhumanly wide, a python preparing to swallow its prey whole. She hissed in Delia's face, bearing her fangs. Delia froze, immobilized by terror at the predatory beast inches away from her. Michelle leaned forward and bit, her razor sharp fangs pierced through shirt and bra and sank into the soft fatty tissue of Delia's right breast. Delia's terror peaked and her bowels released. Urine ran down her legs to pool on the floor beneath her. She gagged, but couldn't vomit as her esophagus was constricted by Michelle's wicked hold on her throat. She swallowed it back down to breathe.

Michelle released Delia's breast, licked the blood off her lips, and held Delia's terrified gaze with murderous intensity. Delia was deathly pale and shaking with a mewling sound—the only noise that could escape her constricted wind pipe.

Time to stop playing around and get serious. She reached her free hand up Delia's skirt and tore off her cotton underwear. Delia squealed at the brush of Michelle's sharp claws across her intimate folds.

Michelle licked her finger tips suggestively, as Delia shook her head back and forth whining, "No, no, nooooooo." She stuck her hand all the way up into Delia's tender flesh, forcing her to accommodate her whole fist. Delia grunted hard as her entire body was pushed upward with the strength of Michelle's thrust. When her hand squeezed all the way in reaching the limit, Michelle tweaked her claws into the flesh around Delia's cervix drawing blood.

Delia's aura flared with a new plateau of pain, terror and humiliation as she realized the horrid mutilation of her body that was about to occur. She cried and bawled like a child.

Michelle looked at her sideways, debating whether she should just do it, or give the girl a chance. She opted for the latter. "I will cut out your uterus and ovaries. Then I will feed them to you. If you still live, I will drain every drop of your blood. Do you doubt me?"

With tears streaming down her face, Delia whimpered, "No." Michelle eased back the tension on Delia's throat to better hear her speak. After several gasping breaths, she begged for her life, sobbing, "I don't wanna die. Please don't kill me. I'll leave New York. I'll never come back. You'll never see me again, I promise. Please have mercy. I don't wanna die like this. I'll do anything you want. Anything!"

Michelle pulled her hand partway out of Delia's bruised flesh and stroked her sensitive clit intimately with her thumb. Delia bucked and squealed as Michelle tweaked and caressed her buttons in a playful mix of pleasure and pain.

She continued begging for her life and freedom. "Please … Oh God … Please … anything you want … just please, let me go …"

Michelle spoke low and cold, barely above a whisper, "You leave the state. I let you have your life and your body—intact. Remember this well. Remember every day of your miserable life that you live by my mercy. You can still bear children by my mercy." Michelle paused, Delia nodded frantically in agreement.

"If I see you, hear of you, or find you have returned, I will hunt you down. There is no place you can hide. And I will make good on my threats." Michelle tweaked her clit once more, a reminder. *"Entendez-moi?* Understand? You need another demonstration?"

Delia shook her head vigorously. "No. Please, no more. I'll leave tonight. Now! You'll never see me again, I swear! Please, please let me go!" She sobbed and groveled with the spark of hope that she could survive this night without being mutilated and scarred for life. Michelle released her and she collapsed to the floor lying in her own urine. Delia bawled in relief, her entire body trembling uncontrollably.

* * * *

Aaron and Michelle said their goodbyes to everyone. Heading towards the door, Kyle caught Aaron and pulled him aside, "Hey, do you have to take off so soon? Delia's gone already. She was real upset. I don't think she'll be back tonight."

Aaron smiled warmly. "I don't think Delia will return, but I've gotta get going. Michelle and I have some other plans."

Kyle nodded in reluctant acceptance, "Hey, did you hear what happened to those two cops that were here looking for you?" Aaron shook his head.

"Yeah, it's fuckin' crazy. They were found dead at a hotel. One guy shoved off the balcony and the other one was torn apart like hamburger. It's been all over the news. You haven't heard about it?"

Aaron grinned. "Yeah, there are some real animals out there. It's pretty dangerous to be a cop these days." Aaron pegged Kyle with a direct stare. Kyle stared back apprehensively.

Aaron read his mind as Kyle briefly entertained the idea that the unfortunate fate of the detectives had something to do with Aaron and Michelle. Kyle couldn't envision either of them as vicious murderers. They were fun, attractive, and charming. No way they could have been involved in such a massacre. No way possible.

Kyle dismissed the thought and clapped Aaron on the back, snickering in a tone of mutual conspiracy. "Well I guess the good news is you don't have to worry about those assholes bothering you anymore."

Aaron and Michelle gave him identical, gleaming white, predatory smiles as they departed, slipping out the door into the New York nightlife.

* * * *

Two days later:

"I think we have worn out our welcome in New York. I don't like the *problème* with the police. Is a very high profile investigation. Good time to travel. Since you have nothing to hold you here, I think we should go." Michelle paused in consideration, "Have you ever been to Europe? Paris, London, Rome?"

He shrugged, and then thought of something. "No, I haven't really been anywhere. You know what Kyle and I had planned? We were gonna do a vacation in Vegas. Never made it there. I'd still like to go."

Michelle kissed him. "*Ooohhh* … I love Las Vegas, the city that never sleeps. Is perfect for vampires, don't you think?"

The End

Coming December 2013

The 5th installment in the Nightlife Series

THE NIGHTLIFE: LONDON

Join Travis Luedke's mailing list for FREE ebooks:

CONTINUE READING FOR MORE NIGHTLIFE SERIES NOVELS

BLOOD SLAVE

Her mother named her Esperanza Salvación – Hope for Salvation. But when a girl works as an escort for Colombian cartel in the ghettos of Spanish Harlem...there wasn't much hope, or salvation.

Hope's telepathic ability keeps her a step ahead of ruin, but her unusual gift attracts the attention of a psychotic vampire bitch. Trapped in a Manhattan penthouse with the psycho, she thought she was dead meat.

Her survival lies in the hands of Vampire Master Enrique. He seems to respect her, perhaps even care. As a measure of protection, he makes her his personal Bloodslave. Helplessly addicted to his bite, Enrique rules her every moment. As always, Hope must adapt to survive.

Swept into the decadent nightlife of Manhattan's elite, she falls in love with Enrique and prays someday he may grow to love her, too. But is it simply a relationship of convenience? Is she nothing more than a concubine desperate to satisfy his nightly demands for blood and sex?

And forever in the background is the fear that one day the cartel boss she abandoned will hunt her down to collect on old debts.

★★★★★ "Fast paced, no holds-barred, gripping, gut-wrenching, soul-ripping and most definitely tear-inducing. Perfection!"

★★★★★ "Travis Luedke writes amazing characters and amazing stories and unbelievable passion flawlessly. After reading this book I was left in shock."

★★★★★ "You know when you see a violent or bloody scene in a movie and you cover your eyes for a couple of seconds until it has past? I caught myself doing that with this book, then I realized that the lines were not going to go away until I read them."

THE NIGHTLIFE LAS VEGAS

Vampires, Aaron Pilan and his master Michelle, live by one rule – no bloodslaves. EVER. Aaron breaks that rule when he meets Anastasia. All Anastasia wants is to be loved and cherished, but the predatory men she's attracted to bring her only pain and abuse. Escaping one train-wreck relationship for another, she finds happiness with Aaron and Michelle as a bloodslave, a 'pet'. When Aaron uses his telepathy to win thousands at the gambling tables, he attracts the deadly attention of the Colombian Cartel and Aaron and Michelle are 'disappeared'. Addicted to the bite of her vampire lovers, Ana is desperate to find them. But, Las Vegas isn't ready for vampires mixing heroin, sex and vengeance. Ana is trapped in the spiraling chaos.

Find out what happens in the second novel of the Nightlife Series.

★★★★★ "Go grab a copy before this much fun is declared illegal."

★★★★★ "Mr. Luedke once again showcasing his considerable talent for crafting erotic, action-packed, supernatural thrillers that leave the reader saying "Wow!""

★★★★★ "A no-holds-barred, easy-to-read romp that mixes fantasy, suspense, horror and erotica, and does it well."

THE NIGHTLIFE PARIS

Vampire master Michelle, and her slave, Aaron Pilan, flee to Paris, leaving behind the slaughter in Las Vegas. Aaron made the costly mistake of taking a bloodslave, and then married her. The tragedy of his wife's death has driven a rift between them and Michelle is desperate to heal the breach.

Struggling with his predatory alter ego, Aaron is fractious, rebelling against his master. He desires another bloodslave, and that Michelle cannot allow. She opens her heart and soul to Aaron and he relives, through her memories, her dark, gritty tale of survival in the savagery of WWII Paris under the German occupation. Michelle's staggering revelations are deeply disturbing. The confrontation of master versus slave comes full circle as the couple faces death and separation.

And they are not alone in Paris. An investigator has followed them from Vegas seeking the unique gifts of Michelle's blood. He's watching and waiting for the opportunity to make his move against them.

Find out what happens in the third novel of the Nightlife Series.

★★★★★ "I was screaming at one point, crying, at another. It was an emotional roller coaster of a book."

★★★★★ "This segment of Michelle and Aaron's tale is dark and graphic, but with mesmerizing descriptions and a morbidly compelling storyline, I felt this was the best of The Nightlife Series by far."

★★★★★ "Decidedly darker and somewhat disturbing, THE NIGHTLIFE: PARIS takes the series for a turn towards the dark side and I loved every minute of it!"

THE NIGHTLIFE SERIES OMNIBUS (BOOKS 1-4)

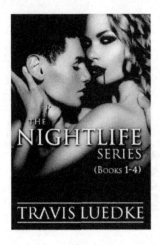

The Nightlife Series is violent, sexy, and occasionally violently sexy.

Vampires, strippers, escorts, night clubs, pimps & dirty cops – the Nightlife Series is never boring.

Can decadence, corruption and prostitution go hand in hand with self-control? Over-indulgence, illegal activity and vampires lurk in darkness when night falls on the city.

The Nightlife Series explores the sexy, dangerous misadventures of vampires and an interesting assortment of wickedly corrupt men and women of the night. Gangs, pimps, prostitutes, cartel, mafia, drug dealers, addicts, alcoholics, all those wonderfully colorful people you find rubbing elbows in the back alleys, night clubs, and strip joints.

These creatures inhabit a world of constant blood, sex, and arousal. The act of feeding is highly erotic, victims often experience multiple orgasms. A vampire's bite is the most powerful drug imaginable, ecstasy, euphoria, and an ever-present potential for addiction. Lethally violent predators, they can cut through flesh like a hot knife through butter. They slip through the nightlife quietly, unobtrusively, until cornered. Then it gets ugly, people die.

The Nightlife Series includes:

THE NIGHTLIFE NEW YORK
THE NIGHTLIFE LAS VEGAS
THE NIGHTLIFE PARIS
BLOOD SLAVE

These wicked, pulse-pounding novels drag readers breathless through one cataclysmic event after another....bite into your copy today!

THE SHEPHERD

Skate punks, kleptomaniacs, clairvoyant visions and reincarnation...

...THE SHEPHERD is unlike any other Young Adult novel you have ever read.

Mike Evans here. Sixteen year old skate punk squatting in a white-trash trailer park with my loser drunk Dad. Seems I lost most of my friends when Dad lost our home in foreclosure. Only Anita stuck by me. Worse, I keep having strange clairvoyant visions of things that always come true.

Then I almost ran over Nadia in my Geo. A passing truck finished the job – left a crumpled heap of skin and bone on the road. I fixed her. Me.

Now this fourteen year old girl won't leave me alone. I sorta let her sneak in my window when she needs a place to crash.

I have a double life: daytime at school, Anita, skating, and then my nights with Nadia. She's my secret friend, gives me money and listens to my problems when nobody else will.

My world is spinning out of control. Old friends have turned enemy, my grisly visions of death won't quit, and Anita's intentions make my head spin. Even with all that, I've got bigger stuff to worry about.

Nadia's hiding something.

★★★★★ "I could not put this book down. All I keep thinking about is what could possibly happen next. I felt as if I was back in high school with them!"

★★★★★ "It's almost a love triangle of epic proportions or so you think....Travis blew me away with this book, I never saw what was coming."

Sharp, witty, dark and gritty, The Shepherd is the must read Young adult paranormal thriller of 2013. Get your copy now!

ABOUT TRAVIS LUEDKE

Travis Luedke is a husband, father, and author of Urban Fantasy Thriller, Paranormal Romance, Contemporary Fantasy, Young Adult Fiction, and Sci-fi. He is currently catching a 3rd degree sunburn in San Antonio, Texas, and loving every minute of it.

As the author of the Nightlife Series novels, Travis lives very vicariously through his writings. He invites you to enjoy his macabre flights of fancy, but be warned: *The Nightlife Series is violent, sexy, and occasionally violently sexy.*

http://www.twluedke.com/

Social Media, & other links
Blog   http://thenightlifeseries.blogspot.com/
Blog   http://twluedke.blogspot.com/
Twitter https://twitter.com/TWLuedke or @TWLuedke
Facebook https://www.facebook.com/TheNightlifeSeries
Goodreads http://www.goodreads.com/TWLuedke
Email twluedke@gmail.com

Made in the USA
Las Vegas, NV
22 January 2023

66072850R00079